Used to being self-reliant, Mary realized she needed to trust someone else.

"Peter," she whispered the name as strong arms reached out to catch her.

"Mary!"

"You are here," she said weakly. "I simply said your name and you appeared."

Peter's worried expression softened and a hint of a smile played at his lips. "'Tis my lot, milady. Rescuing fair maids who have no one else to champion them." He lifted her easily into his arms. "You must rest now, Mary."

Mary nodded and allowed her head to fall back against his chest. How good it felt to rest. How good it felt to be held and cared for.

Mary was asleep before Peter could get her to a bed. He worried that she suffered from more than exhaustion, but seeing no sign of fever or swelling, he relaxed a bit.

She is beautiful, he thought, sweeping back ebony ringlets from her face. Her wild dark hair, tied simply at the nape of her neck, gave her a gypsy look. Peter could not tear himself away from her. Instead, he held her hand for a moment and wondered at the woman who had so selflessly cared for everyone else. Who was she? She dressed simply enough, but the cloak upon her bed revealed quality in its design, and the shoes upon her feet were nearly new.

The daughter of a physician, he remembered and wondered why she had introduced herself thusly, when she was obviously a wife or perhaps widow, and mother besides.

"Who are you, little Mary?" he whispered, before laying her hand gently across her waist. "And why have ye vexed me so sorely?"

Tracie J. Peterson is a popular inspirational writer from Kansas. Tracie has also written eight successful **Heartsong Presents** titles under the name of Janelle Jamison. *If Only* reflects Tracie's love for history and research.

HEARTSONG PRESENTS

Don't miss out on any of our super romances. Write to us at the following address for information on our newest releases and club information.

Heartsong Presents Readers' Service
P.O. Box 719
Uhrichsville, OH 44683

If Only

Tracie J. Peterson

Heartsong Presents

A note from the Author:
*I love to hear from my readers! You may correspond
with me by writing:*

Tracie J. Peterson
Author Relations
P.O. Box 719
Uhrichsville, OH 44683

ISBN 1-55748-968-8

IF ONLY

Cover illustration by Brian Bowman.

PRINTED IN THE U.S.A.

prologue

England, 1349

The bubonic plague has wrecked havoc upon all of Europe. In England, over one-third of the population is dead or dying from the dread disease. In its wake, the plague has left entire families dead, whole villages burned, and vital records of both destroyed for all time. This dark, macabre age would haunt generations to come.

As people mourned their losses, an anguished cry rose from the depths of their souls. . .if only. If only we knew what caused this grave disease. If only we could save the lives waning before us. If only we had not sinned and caused such devastation to be rained down upon us. If only. . .

one

Mary Elizabeth Beckett crouched behind the kitchen screen in hopes her father would not spy her out. *'Twould be a pity to miss out on this,* she thought.

Guy Beckett, oblivious to his daughter's whereabouts, directed his two colleagues into the house. He motioned them past the kitchen to the small, dark corner room. Here, Guy Beckett performed his experiments and looked for the elusive answers to questions that vexed him regarding the human body and medicine.

"Be careful with it," he instructed the men. They carried a large trunk of considerable weight and only grunted a reply of acknowledgment.

Mary's excitement urged her to peek out from the screen as the men cautiously made their way into the secluded room. A dull thud told her that the trunk had reached its destination.

"You are sure no one saw you?" Guy questioned his friends.

"We are as much at risk as you," stated one. Mary knew this man to be a fellow physician of her father's.

"Aye, 'twould not bode well for us to be caught with this baggage in hand," the other, a stranger to Mary, said with a wave of his hand over the trunk.

When the door closed, Mary sprang up with a lightning step from her hiding place and hurried up into the loft. Her room was directly over her father's workshop, and for many years she had peered down to watch his actions. *He will not mind*, she thought, certain that her father knew full well of her observations. And why not? Mary worked hard at his side and loved healing the sick as much as he did. He would only see this curiosity as one more part of her training.

Gently, so that she would not disturb the procedures in the room below, Mary lifted the knothole in her plank floor and eased down to place her eye against the opening.

"He's quite a puny fellow," her father was saying.

She watched as the three men laid out the body on her father's work table. Her heart raced in the realization that her father was about to perform a much forbidden dissection.

"He was from the prison. Died just this morning," the other physician was saying. Mary waited for some further comment about the cadaver, but none came.

"What news do you bring from Paris?" her father asked his friend.

"The news is much the same as it is here. The Italian Fever has nearly emptied the halls of our great university. Many of your old acquaintances are gone, ravaged by the terrible disease. 'Tis sheer madness, and the horror of it is enough to make me risk the church's disapproval and—"

"And death," the third man added. "Whether it comes by the hand of the church or this destructive disease—'tis certain one or the other will claim us."

Guy Beckett nodded. "They think to frighten us with reproaches of hell for the single action of seeking to know the human body better."

"I have seen the likes of hell," the man replied. "'Tis in France. Marseilles is deserted. So many lives were lost last year, there were scarcely enough left to bury the dead. Nearly all those who remain have suffered one malady or another."

"'Tis rapidly turning that way here in England," Guy stated with deep sorrow. "As the weather has warmed, more and more cases are evident, and yet by what means? We have so little knowledge regarding this matter, and clearly there is nothing in the handful of books available to me."

"Feel not at loss for this. There is nothing in Paris either. We have concluded, however, 'tis most likely a planetary conjunction. In the year of our Lord 1345, March the twentieth to be exact, the planets of Saturn, Mars, and Jupiter were aligned. 'Tis well documented."

"I heard our good colleague Doctor Dupré speak of this. He believed it to have corrupted the atmosphere," Guy replied.

"Aye, but alas our friend has also succumbed to this plague," his friend added.

Mary ached for her father. He had tried so hard to save the villagers from this sickness, and now he had lost another good friend. There seemed to be no reason for the illness. It struck young and old, rich or poor. It mattered not who you were. The plaguing fever with its horrible blackening marks came just the same.

"You will take down what we find here," Mary's father stated. She saw him reach across the table with one of his ledgers. There was no way of knowing to whom he had just directed his order, but Mary presumed it to be the unknown third man.

Since she had been a child, Mary had worked alongside her father to learn about illnesses and healing. Her father had studied at the University of Paris and was quite knowledgeable in the field of medicine. Many came to seek his advice, and often the scene that set itself below her was repeated with other friends and fellow learners. He had a great craving for knowledge, especially the knowledge to save human lives. It was a passion for her father. It was a passion for Mary, as well.

"See here," her father's muffled voice stated from behind

a bird-like mask. Physicians had taken to wearing the masks when working on the truly ill. Because of this they were often called beak doctors. "The buobon area shows the engorged nodes."

Mary remembered from her Greek studies that buobon meant groin. Frustrated that she couldn't view this part of the dead man's body, Mary concentrated on the man's neck and upper torso, noting the swollen glands there as well. It was certainly the bubonic plague, she surmised, although only physicians called it so.

She wondered how rapidly the disease had claimed its victim. Some people went to bed perfectly healthy one night and never woke up again. Others lingered for days and died in bizarre, frenzied terror. Mary shuddered and tried to concentrate on her father's voice. She had to learn as much as she could or she would be no help to the people around her.

Her father was just making a long incision in the man's abdomen when a loud ruckus broke out in the night. Angry shouts filtered up to her room, causing Mary to spring to her feet and dart to her window. Easing the shutter back, she peered into the dark.

"Come out, Beckett. Yer doin' the devil's work. 'Tis an unholy thing, and we mean to be no part of it!" Mary recognized the voice of the village butcher.

Another voice joined the first. "You cursed us all, and now our children be dyin' from the fever. God has cursed us because of you!"

"No," Mary moaned and leaned back from the window. What would happen if the villagers stormed the house and found the cadaver? They blamed her father for not having the answers to the disease which claimed more lives daily. They eyed him suspiciously because neither he nor his daughter had fallen ill from the plague. Now they formed an angry mob, and there would be no reasoning with them.

Mary hurried downstairs to warn her father, but he was already approaching the door. "Get thee to safety, child," he whispered and motioned her away from the door.

"I will not see you harmed," she cried and felt the rough hands of the stranger move her away from her father.

"We will go with him," the man assured her, and Mary could only nod and allow it to happen.

The three men went outside to meet the crowd, while Mary wondered what possible good she could do. Voices raised in anger. The hatred startled her, but not more than the people's despair. From the background came a wailing of women who no doubt had lost more loved ones than they could bear, and Mary felt their heartache as fiercely as if it were her own. Had she not nursed their sick children? Had she not seen them die one after the other?

The sound of rocks being thrown at the house sobered Mary. What was she to do? What could she do?

Hurrying from the front room, Mary made her way to her father's workshop. She pulled out a large traveling bag and began to fill it with bottles of medicinal herbs and instruments. The crude assortment was limited, but important, and Mary could not let it fall into the wrong hands. Neither, she thought, could she allow her father's years of hard work fade away. If the very worst were to happen this night, she would be the only hope of keeping her father's studies alive. She pulled open the cupboard where her father kept his journals and hurriedly gathered them.

The noise outside grew louder. Calls for killing the trio struck terror in Mary's heart. Suddenly she knew there was no hope of ever seeing her father again. She crammed the journals into the bag, added whatever else looked useful, and hoisted the bag to her shoulders.

Escaping the madness was all she could think of, but when Mary moved toward the door, her gaze fell upon the face of the dead man. He was younger than she'd thought him to be. How sad that he should die so horribly. Without thought as to why she did it, Mary reached down and pulled a linen cloth over the body. Somehow she felt comforted by this simple act. Somehow it seemed the only normal thing to do in the midst of such chaos.

Taking her cloak, Mary slipped out the back door. She could still hear her father trying to reason with his neighbors and thought for a moment that she might go to his aid.

"'Tis a natural fear you have, but anger will not heal your children. You must return to your homes and allow me to come and bring you medicines."

"Your medicine may well be the death of us," a woman cried. "My child lived and breathed before you and your witch of a daughter came to my house with your precious potions."

At that comment, Mary realized she would be less than welcome should she appear at her father's side. She raged within at the thought that these people, once friends, could be so blind in their superstitions. *If only they could see the truth,* she thought sadly.

Forcing herself into the dark cover of the forest, Mary watched the scene play itself out. "Witch, indeed," she muttered. "Just because I find no value in the babblings of the priest and work to learn healing alongside my father, they think me a witch."

As if having heard Mary's thoughts, another woman screeched through the noise. "Ye be indentured to the Devil, hisself. I have seen with my own eyes."

"What say you to that?" the butcher shouted to Guy Beckett.

"I am innocent of such a charge, as are my good colleagues and daughter. I seek to learn of the human body in order to heal it. Nothing more. Nothing less."

"'Tis a heretic, he is," the woman yelled. "He mutilates the flesh of the dead!"

"Heretic! Heretic!" the cry went up from the masses.

They stormed the house, taking Guy and the other two men with them. Mary noted that the third man was only moved from his place after several villagers took hold of him.

There was no sense in lingering, Mary knew. She slipped deeper into the woods and made her way to the top of the hillside where she hoped she could somehow view the fate of her father and home. The mob would find the cadaver, and the priest himself would see the house burned to the ground. No reasoning, no amount of pleading could bring her father back from certain death.

Struggling with the bag, she wiped away tears and pushed forward. She had just made the top of the hill when the house erupted into flames.

"No!" she cried, clutching the bag to her breast. Her cloak caught the wind and billowed out behind her. "'Tis not fair, God!" she shook her fist to the sky. "You have never been for me or him! Now he is dead. Is that Your price? You have taken him from me, and now I am alone. Where comes the justice or good in that?"

The villagers were chanting and raging at the burning house. It was more than Mary could bear to witness, and without a second glance over her shoulder, she pushed on into the night and the sheltering haven of thick English forest.

The moon was well into the western skies when Mary stopped running. Pain wove its way through her body, making breathing almost impossible. Everything hurt, but she wanted it to. The numbness in her heart threatened to consume her body. She wanted to hurt, wanted to feel anything rather than lose herself in emptiness.

Mary fell upon the ground and cried in agony. Nothing

had prepared her for the death of her father. Nothing she'd experienced in the wake of the plague had terrified her as did this night.

What should she do? Where could she go? Most of her father's friends were in Paris, and she had no coin to make her way there. Her mother, long dead in child-bearing, had no kin, and other than her father's mother, a woman he despised for her religious rhetoric, she had no one.

Feeling her breathing steady, Mary forced herself to sit. She could see nothing but black empty spaces and knew she was a great distance from the next village.

"I dare not go anywhere I am known," she muttered aloud. "If they know me not to be dead, they will simply seek to finish the job."

She clutched the bag close to her and scoffed at her own foolishness. "'Tis a sorry pilgrim I am," she mused. No food, no coin. Only a bag filled with herbal remedies, useless instruments, and her father's medical journals.

"Your grandmother sought her beliefs, and I sought mine," Mary remembered her father saying. "She believed her God could produce miracles just like that." He had snapped his fingers before Mary's eyes.

"But why do we never journey to see her?"

Her father had shrugged his shoulders. "Most likely she would not have us. I scoffed at her God and chose a more valid means of study. Science. When I left for the university, she was greatly disappointed in me."

"Then she forbade you to come home?" Mary had questioned.

"Nay, I forbade myself."

The memory faded, leaving Mary more lonely than ever. She had only one choice. She would go north and seek out her grandmother. All she remembered was that Lady Beckett lived near York. Surely that small knowledge would be enough to help Mary find her. Then a terrible thought crossed Mary's mind. Her father had not been a young man. Surely his own mother would be dead by now, if not by old age, then from the plague fever.

"'Tis the only choice I have," Mary reasoned. "I cannot go back. I must go forward. Mayhap my grandmother will welcome me."

Clouds gathered overhead and blocked out the little bit of moonlight. Foreboding overtook Mary, causing her to draw her knees to her chest with the bag lodged awkwardly between. She pulled the cloak tight as if to ward off the uneasy sensations.

"'Tis sorry I am, Father. I know you'd not want me going to grandmother's home. I have naught but this and can see no other way. Please do not be angry with me."

She rocked back and forth, tenderly stroking the bag, feeling the presence of her father in his last earthly possessions. Somehow she would find the strength to go on. Somehow she would take her father's work forward and use his understanding to help others.

Succumbing to her misery, Mary slumped to the ground and rolled into a ball around the bag. She had to go on for the sake of the only man she had ever loved. If only she could make it to her grandmother's home, all would certainly be well.

two

Sir Peter Donne had always been popular among the ladies and gambling houses. He'd known his fair share of time with both and never missed a chance to grab the best life had to offer. From the unruly brown curls which met the collar of his tunic to the well-trimmed mustache and beard, Peter Donne was all man and all charm.

He was a head taller than most men, and his shoulders were broad and thick with muscle. He'd spent his years since turning ten and five in service to King Edward III of England, and now after seven years of such devotion to king and country, Peter had come home.

But 'twas a changed England to which the man returned, and in like, 'twas a changed man who returned to England. Gone was the cocky youth who had charmed and lied his way across Europe. Gone, too, was the wit and roguish behavior. Peter had seen too much death and too many horrors.

Stepping onto the dock, he glanced around him and noted the faces colored by fear and anguish. It was the same wherever he went. Most of Europe had seen thousands dead from the dreaded plague, and now he could see that the same was true of England. Already he smelled the stench of death. Where would it end?

Part of him wanted nothing more than to get back on the ship and sail away. But where could one sail to escape the terror of everyday life? No, his allegiance to Edward demanded that he stay. Besides, running away from a fight had never been Peter's style.

15

He pressed on, passing the scant crew of dock workers and fishmongers. Most seemed to eye him with relative disinterest, but occasionally a surprised man would look up to see the regal king's man in his short tunic of braided leather over dark wool and hose. His well-muscled legs betrayed his athletic prowess, and no one who observed him doubted that there was still a good fight left in Peter Donne. But more than that, Peter represented health and prosperity—something many folks only dreamed of these days.

Moving away from the docks, he wound his way through the narrow city streets. Here between the shops and alleyways, people moved with single-minded purpose. Some held posy bouquets to ward off the smell, while others simply used rags to cover their mouths and noses. Peter grimaced at the stench, but did neither. It had been the same in France.

The same stricken look had crossed the channel to mar the faces of the English as well. Crying could be heard in the streets and, as Peter moved deeper into the populated sections of town, he found the sight he'd most dreaded to see. The plague dead themselves lay in wait upon the curb for the body collectors to bury them in mass.

Such scenes had stolen Peter's youth from him. This horror of everyday life caused him to consider each waking moment with question and sleep away each night in unspoken terror.

He forced himself to ignore the dead. He could do naught for them, and the smell, so overpowering even without the added discomfort of seeing the corpses, caused Peter to hasten his step. But where could he go? There was no place to avoid this confrontation. Even the houses were marked with crucifixes and the words, "Lord have mercy on us."

A filthy beggar woman approached Peter and cried out, "Alms, for food. Alms, sire, please."

Peter eyed her cautiously. He'd thought her quite old when she'd first approached him, but as she stretched her hand out to his face, he realized she wasn't much older than he was. He reached into a small bag on his belt and produced a coin. It wasn't much, but the woman blessed him for it and offered him a charm to keep him from the plague. It was little more than a rotten piece of cloth, but she swore it had been blessed by the archbishop and that it would keep him from evil.

Peter nodded and hastened away from the woman. When he'd crossed the alleyway and was well out of sight, he tossed the material to the cobblestone street and tried to forget the pain-stricken look in the woman's eyes.

"Lookin' for a warm bed, luv?" a voice called from a nearby doorway.

Peter looked up to find another haggard woman. This one also sought to make a coin, but not in the manner of the first. "Nay, 'tis no rest for the likes of me," he said, trying to sound good-natured. The woman shrugged her shoulders and let him pass without further comment.

Where had all the beauty gone? he wondered. Were there no charming ladies in velvets and satins to feast his eyes upon? And if there were, would he find any comfort in their presence? Once such diversion would have been uppermost in his mind, but now 'twas a distant memory of another time . . .another man.

Peter picked up his pace. At this rate his squire and armor would precede him to the king. Reaching King Edward suddenly became Peter's focus. He'd summoned Peter from France and beckoned him to make haste. The matter troubled Peter, but he would not share his concerns with his squire or any of their other traveling companions. If Edward sought him for a task, Peter would take the duty on with honor and be true to his knights' calling. Still, Peter knew he had little heart for any task. How could he give himself over to any job when the issue of his own mortality refused to be pushed aside? *Will duty and honor mourn me when I am dead and gone?* Peter wondered. Had he wasted his life upon the battlefield, fighting against a people who had never wronged him?

So many things had been clear before this confounded sickness had taken the world captive. At one time, Peter had known what he wanted from life. *Now,* he thought with a harsh laugh, *I have no thought for life because death consumes my time.* Staring with hard, cold eyes at the madness around him, Peter realized that death was consuming much more than time.

Arriving at the palace, Peter was confronted by King Edward's chamberlain. "His majesty refuses to be disturbed by anyone," the short, squat man told Peter.

"Is he ill?"

"Certainly not!" The man seemed surprised by Peter's question.

Patience had never served well at Peter's side. "What then is to be my task?"

"His Majesty wishes you to go out upon the land. You will take this," the man handed Peter a thin parcel, "to the abbey outside of York. I will give you the name of the abbott and a letter of introduction."

"For this I returned to England?" Peter's surprise was clear. "Have you no other errand boys?"

"Aye, but His Majesty called for you." The chamberlain was indignant at Peter's questioning. "His Majesty requires a greater service of you. You are to take account of the devastation upon the land. As you pass on your way to York, the king desires that you make a written account. In each monastery and town you will seek out those in authority and learn the numbers of their dead."

"Am I to go alone?"

"Aye, there are scarcely enough in service here to send you with an army." The chamberlain took advantage of his station and pressed the issue. "You are to move swiftly and be not hindered by even so much as your squire."

"But I have need of my squire," Peter protested. Things were definitely not going the way he'd hoped.

"The king has need of him here. You are to be given a swift horse, provisions for the journey, and this." The man dropped a small bag of coins upon the table. "There is enough money here to meet any need you may have."

"Money?" Peter laughed at this strange turn of events. While money still held its power, it meant so little in the face of sickness. It could not buy a cure. With so many already dead, the fields went untended and food was fast becoming scarce. For those who had something to eat, no amount of coin could entice it away. One could not eat silver and gold.

The chamberlain had clearly reached the limits of his tolerance. "I will inform His Majesty that you are well on your way."

Peter locked eyes with the man for a moment. He saw both fear and longing within the older man's gaze. *How alike we are*, Peter thought. Both of them were questioning the sense of this trip, but neither could speak on the matter and neither had a choice about whether it would take place.

Peter picked up the bag, added it to his belt, and nodded. "The journey should prove tedious, nevertheless I will endeavor to fulfill my duties. Give the King my word of honor on the matter."

Peter happily left the city, not because of the task before him, but because of his desire to escape the sights that lay before his eyes. The city that had once nurtured him, now smothered him and drained his strength. He knew the roads would be congested with pilgrims and other travelers, but on horseback he could move faster than most and soon he would leave all of them behind. Perhaps the open country-side would relieve him of the growing burden in his heart.

But the burden only grew as Peter stared into the faces of his fellow travelers. They all seemed to ask each other, "Why am I here? And to where should I go?"

Peter had contemplated like questions for many miles. His youth made him eager to work, but he'd grown weary of killing and destroying. Where man left off dispensing death, the plague had pushed ahead. The sickness had spread from Italy, to France, and now to England. There was little hope of escaping its effects, yet the people on the road were proof enough of the desire to try.

Peter slowed his mount to a trot and noted another band of travelers ahead on the road. They all wanted to forget what lay in the city, but where could any of them go to erase those memories? There were so many questions. If only there were answers.

The first night of his journey found Peter taking refuge in a rundown ale house. The proprietor showed him to a sectioned-off room and pointed to a straw-filled mattress. Exhaustion so claimed him that Peter completely ignored the stench of previous use and fell into a deep sleep.

The next night found him better off, barely making it in time to pass through the Trumpington Gate into Cambridge. People eyed him suspiciously but moved out of his way.

He reined back on the horse in front of the Red Boar Inn. It looked to be a decent enough place to stay. Peter paid a young boy to care for his horse and offered him another coin if he had the horse waiting for him at dawn's first light. The boy, a filthy child who looked as though he slept his nights in the stable as well, happily complied.

Peter grabbed his things and hurried inside the inn. His

body ached from the long hours upon the trail and his stomach growled in protest at the aroma of stew and fresh bread.

"Be needin' a room, milord?" the innkeeper asked.

"First a meal, then a room," Peter replied, running a hand through his sweat-soaked hair. "Perhaps a bath?"

"For coin, me wife can fill a kettle for ye, but we have no tub."

"I will pay extra for a tub." The words surprised the proprietor, as well as Peter. He'd not thought about a bath until that moment, but now the idea consumed him. He tossed a coin to the innkeeper, and immediately the man became devoted to Peter's needs.

"Ye can count on me to see to it, milord. Let it ne're be said the Red Boar could not care for its own." He turned from Peter to call out, "Josiah!"

A boy of about twelve appeared in the doorway. "Aye, Father?"

"Take the tub to the room at the top of the stairs. Then see to it that ye fill it with hot water. Leave two bucketfuls besides." The boy nodded and hurried to do his father's bidding.

"No tub, eh?" Peter said with a hint of a smile. He'd learned early on that things were seldom what they appeared.

"'Tis not often requested," the innkeeper said with a shrug. "I forget its existence at times."

From the smell of the man, Peter knew he spoke the truth. "I want food brought to the room. Here." he tossed the man another coin and watched as his eyes grew large. It was twice the price he'd thought to ask. "Later, I will desire to speak with you privately."

"As ye wish, milord." The man hurried to show Peter to the room and nearly knocked his son down when the boy rushed through the doorway.

Water sloshed out from the buckets, but was quickly

soaked up by the dry plank boards of the floor. Deep cracks from years of wear seemed to suck up the liquid as though it were a thirsty dog lapping water. Peter tossed his provisions bag to the small bed and began to remove his clothes. After two more trips, the boy had sufficiently filled the tub and Peter waved him away when he returned with two more buckets of steaming water.

"'Tis enough, leave them and go."

The boy dropped the buckets beside the tub and hurried out of the room. He'd no sooner gone, however, when a knock came upon the door, and Peter, wearing only his woolen hose, opened it to find the innkeeper.

"Me missus sent these, milord." The man held up a linen towel and sliver of soap.

"Thank your good woman for me," Peter said with only a hint of irritation in his voice. He turned to close the door, but the man held out his hand.

"I have yer food, as well." He reached down to the floor and brought up a tray.

Peter's stomach growled loudly at the sight of the thick stew, bread, and drink. "Again, my thanks." This time the man did nothing to stop him from closing the door.

Peter put the tray beside the tub, grabbed a chunk of the bread, and dipped it into the bowl. With one hand he filled his mouth and with the other he discarded his hose. Steam from the bath beckoned him, and with one fluid movement, Peter immersed himself in the water, still chewing the stew-soaked bread.

He lost track of time. Soaking in the tub seemed to ease away the memories of the past few weeks. It had been a great many weeks since he'd enjoyed a hot bath and a real bed. With the penetrating heat soothing his tired muscles, Peter began to forget about the outside world and concentrated only on his food and bath. Perhaps there were still some pleasures in life.

Hours later, the innkeeper returned and, with Peter's nod of approval, commanded his son to remove the tub and empty tray.

"Ye wished to speak with me?" The man seemed nervous, and Peter couldn't help but smile.

"That I did, my good man. I am about the king's business."

At this the man's eyes nearly bugged out of his head. "The king himself? 'Tis a fine day when this sorry lot keeps company with one of the king's own men."

Peter nodded. "'Tis my hope you will aid me in my duties."

"Anything."

"I will be traveling about the town tomorrow. 'Tis the king's desire that I account for the dead and the number of sick among your town. I will need a guide, perhaps your son. What was his name?"

"Josiah, milord, and he would be happy to assist ye. Why he knows this town like the rats themselves."

"Good. I must go to the churches."

"There be thirteen parish churches," the man responded with genuine eagerness. "Ye'll hear that for yerself in the morn. The bells will ring morrow-Mass, and such a ruckus could wake the dead."

Peter nodded. The man no doubt had forgotten that Peter, under service to the king, would have heard just such a ruckus in London and any other number of cities before coming to Cambridge.

"I can send Josiah in the morning."

Peter dug into the bag on his belt and produced another coin. "Take this for your trouble. The boy will be with me throughout the day."

"Aye!" the man exclaimed with a bow. "Will ye hang your

shield upon our door?"

Peter knew it was customary for persons of importance to place some symbol of their arrival outside the inn door. He, however, had little interest in announcing his presence and shook his head. "Nay, 'twill not serve either of us for good. I leave on the morrow after making my inquiries."

"Ye cannot hope to do it all in one day. Mayhap another night here. . ."

"Nay. I will leave on the morrow. Speak naught of this to anyone."

Peter showed the older man out and fell across the bed without even bothering to undress.

three

Mary hesitated at the sight of a small band of travelers. She longed for human companionship, yet she feared recognition. What if one of the villagers traveled among those she joined? With a sigh, she stared down from her hillside perch and contemplated what she should do.

"Ho! There on the hill."

Mary's head snapped up, realizing that one of the men below was addressing her. Slowly she got to her feet. It seemed her decision had been made for her.

"'Er ye going north?" the man asked.

Mary slowly made her way down the slippery, dew-coated hillside before answering. "Aye, I am bound for York." She looked the sorry lot over, counting five in the group. One, the only woman, was evidently heavy with child.

"Ye can join up with our band," the man offered. "We be bound for the north as well. We seek the Lady of the Moors."

"Who?"

"Have ye not heard of her?" Mary shook her head and clutched her bag close. The man seemed genuinely surprised at this. He scratched his filthy chin and smiled. He was missing several teeth. "Well, 'tis no matter. Yer welcome to travel with us."

Mary eyed the group more closely. The four men were filthy, and the woman was no better. They had evidently traveled for some time by the looks of their ragged shoes. Then again, Mary realized, those were most likely the only shoes these people had known for some time. How strange she must look to them. She wore new shoes and a warm woolen cloak which had cost her father a tidy sum.

"My father is dead," she offered, seeing them stare at her in unspoken questions. "I would greatly appreciate traveling with you. I can make myself useful, as well."

"How so?" the leader of the group questioned.

Mary pulled the bag out. "I am a healer. I will act as midwife to this fine woman when her time comes."

"Ye be a healer?" one of the other men questioned.

"Aye, 'tis true enough. My father was a great man of medicine. I learned at his side."

The band looked at her for a moment as if trying to decide if she spoke the truth or not. Finally the leader broke into another smile. "'Twill be a pleasure then to have ye join us. To be sure, this woman will have need of ye. Her husband died a fortnight past." Mary gave the woman what she hoped was a sympathetic look. "Her name is Grace. This here be Ralph," the man pointed to a younger version of himself. "He is my son. And this be Edward and Galdren of Bristol. They are brothers."

"And who are you?" Mary questioned.

"I am James of Southhampton."

"I am Mary," she offered, refusing to add anything else.

The man glanced heavenward. "We'd best be off. The day is passing fast."

Mary traveled in silenced, wondering at the devotion her companions felt for the mystical Lady of the Moors. They spoke of her with such reverence that Mary was hard pressed to not question them about this woman's existence. She sounded more the stuff of legends and fireside stories than a flesh-and-blood person.

For the most part, however, Mary simply kept her thoughts to herself, believing that her silence would serve her best. She was now a great distance from home, with nearly a week having passed since the night of her father's death. It was certain that these people would have no knowledge of her. After all, they were from cities well removed from her village, and none had so much as raised an eyebrow in question of her.

The hardest thing for Mary remained the uncertainty of where she was to go. Should she be unable to find her grandmother, what hope would there be? Her skills at healing would not keep her fed, for there were doctors throughout England. Men, well respected and some not so well thought of, were stingy with their practice. A woman would not find a welcome in the business of medicine. She could present herself as a midwife or herbalist, but her claim to anything more would be ignored.

"'Er you alone in this world?" Grace asked her. They traveled side by side, Mary keeping pace with Grace's slow, lumbering strides. The men were well ahead of them, and it suited both women quite well.

"Aye," Mary replied. "I have a grandmother, but she may be dead by now."

Grace nodded. "I have no one." She ran her hand over her swollen belly. "No one but the child."

"When is the child's time?" Mary questioned.

"Soon," Grace replied, her brows knitting together in worry. "'Twas my hope to reach the moor country before delivering."

"You needn't fear," Mary said, trying to offer reassurance. "I have delivered many a child into the world."

"You? But ye look to be a child yerself."

Mary wanted to laugh. She did not feel like a child. Fear, exhaustion, sorrow, and anguish had joined to age her at least ten years.

"My father was a physician. He was a great man, and I worked at his side." Mary's wistful tone betrayed her pain. "I wanted to learn to heal, but of course," she glanced around as though sharing some great secret, "as a woman, it will never be allowed."

"Aye," Grace nodded. "I cannot boast such knowledge. I be a simple woman. My husband died of the fever, and a more hideous death I have yet to witness. He was a weaver by trade, and we knew a good life." Grace's eyes misted over, and Mary felt the compelling urge to reach out and pat her arm. Something inside, however, kept her from offering the comfort.

"This be our firstborn," Grace continued. Her tone took on a new air, one of love and bittersweet joy. "'Tis all I have now of my Gabe. I pray 'tis a boy with red hair like his father."

Mary smiled sadly, and this time she did reach out to touch Grace. "I am certain 'twill be a fine son or daughter, no matter which." Grace sniffed back tears and said nothing more.

That night while sharing a meager supper of roasted hare, Mary listened to the tales woven by James regarding the Lady of the Moors. The group evidently thought the Lady a saint or angel in human form, and their praise of her was unrelenting.

"'Tis said she speaks directly with God."

Mary scoffed at James's words. "Would not the church consider that heresy?"

James pushed back his greasy black hair and considered Mary's statement. "The Lady is no heretic. She may well be a saint."

"Mayhap she is a heavenly visitor," Edward offered.

"Aye, God Hisself may have put her here to help in our time of need. Mayhap she has been blessed with special power."

Mary shook her head. "I doubt seriously that this woman is capable of the great miracles on which you base your journey. 'Tis possible the woman does not even exist. You know this country runs full into its cups with stories and legends of old. Mayhap this great Lady of the Moors is yet another example."

"Nay!" James said adamantly. "She performs miracles. I have heard it told with my own ears."

"Yet you have never witnessed the same, have you?"

Mary's words seemed not to discourage the determined man. "'Tis of no matter what I have or haven't seen. I have the faith to believe 'tis true. That is enough to make me journey north."

"I suppose each person needs something to believe in," Mary said thoughtfully.

"And what do you believe in, mistress?"

Mary shook her head. "I wish I knew. I have seen cruelty at the hands of those who spout superstitious rhetoric and religious litany."

"Surely you do not doubt the church," Galdren spoke up.

Mary laughed. "I do not see that the church has kept England from the plague. Nor do I see where God's mercy is evident in the same." Bitterness edged her voice. "I may be burned alive for my doubts, but better to be honest in the face of death than live a lie."

The group stared at her in silence for a moment. Finally Grace put out her hand and spoke. "'Tis only your great sorrow which causes you to speak thusly. God is still merciful, and though we be an evil people, well deserving of far worse, 'tis He alone who can aid us now."

Mary stared at the woman for several seconds before shaking her head. "I cannot believe God merciful in the face of this terror. Have you not seen the people? Have you not heard their cries and known their fears? You lost your husband to the plague—did he not writhe in the horror of it? Did you not stare into his eyes and see death itself stare back?"

Mary knew her words were cruel, but she couldn't seem to stop their flow. "All of you are hypocrites to call God merciful. If He cared so much, would He not at least spare the children? But, no, they are harder hit yet by the sickness and they suffer too, from the loss of their parents. They are left behind to starve to death, when no one lives to care for them." Mary got to her feet. "I see no mercy. Seek your Lady of the Moors if you must, but fault me not for my disbelief."

She walked away from the group seething in her misery. How could they so calmly speak of God and His mercy? How could they put faith in One who had done nothing to prove Himself worthy of faith?

"Mary." It was Grace. "Mary, I know ye are hurting and 'tis sorry I am that your loss so consumes ye."

Mary turned to face the woman. Set against the distant glow of the campfire, she couldn't see Grace's features, but knew the kindness in her voice. "I am sorry for letting my temper better me."

"I know," Grace said, taking another step forward. "Mary, I have a favor to ask and I know I have no right."

"What is it?"

"Yer words caused me to think, and I fear for my child. If I should die, there is no one who will tend to its needs. Mary, would ye take the babe and see it cared for? I could not bear to leave this world knowing that my own would suffer as those ye described."

Mary instantly felt guilty for her outburst. *Poor Grace. 'Twas bad enough to be with child at a time of such great suffering and horror, but I have doubled her burden by painting a picture of hopelessness for the future, as well.*

"Grace, you will not die. I had no right to put such fear in your heart."

"'Tis not a fear for me. I feel confident of my heavenly home, but the earthy one in which my babe might have to live is a frightful thought. For without a single soul to watch over him, he will die a painful death."

Mary could no longer bear the woman's worried tone. "I

do not believe anything will happen to you, but if it eases your mind, I will care for the child if you should die."

"Thank you, Mary," Grace's words came out with a sob. "I thank God ye have come."

Mary shook her head and watched the woman struggle back down to the camp. *She thanks God for me? What absurdity, for I have done nothing but strain her mind and worry her heart. How could she thank God for one such as I?*

᙮

Peter was mortified at the mounting number of deaths he recorded in his ledger. He had seen death upon the battlefield and watched good friends die within arm's reach, but this disease was something he could not understand. At least a known enemy could be faced and dealt with, but this enemy crept in unannounced and there seemed no way of defense.

He made his way alone, detesting the sights and sounds that assailed him, realizing with each and every step that death might well await him at the next turn.

The sun, high overhead, beat down on him, causing great beads of sweat to roll down his face. The leather cotehardie clung to the under tunic, making his chest feel bound and uncomfortable. Urging his horse into a brief gallop, Peter relished the breeze it created and ignored the pounding ache the jostling ride created in his head.

He approached the village of Byrnbough and reined back his horse to find that there was no village. Not in the true sense. Many of the buildings were nothing more than charred remains, while the houses and shops which stood bore no sign of life. An eerie feeling settled over Peter as he nudged the horse forward. He stared in complete disbelief at the ghostly sight.

Where were the people? Where were the shopkeepers? Did none remain to greet the day?

The horse whinnied nervously, sensing the destruction

and oddity around him. Peter gave his mount a reassuring pat, wishing silently that he might find some reassurance for himself. The small village had once been home to some two hundred souls, but now only emptiness and silence held residence.

Peter brought the horse to halt at the small church in the center of the village. There seemed to be some notice tacked to the door and Peter quickly dismounted and tethered his horse in order to take a look.

"To those souls who may pass this way, know now on this day that the village of Byrnbough is no more. May God have mercy on our souls." Peter read the note twice to make certain he understood. Had the plague claimed the entire village?

He scouted the remains and found nothing but graves and deserted homes. Returning to his horse, Peter took out his ledger and wrote down that the entirety of Byrnbough had been either deserted or given over to the plague.

Pressing on, he found the scenario repeated twice more in smaller villages. The reality of it all caused him to feel light-headed. He, a knight of the king, a man who'd done battle in Crecy but three years past, was nearly undone by the deafening silence of forsaken towns.

Death seemed to stretch its bony fingers closer at every stop. Each time, Peter sensed his own life ebbing away. What madness was this? He had gone nearly two days without a single soul to talk to. Would he find nothing but the same ahead of him?

He prepared to leave the latest scene of devastation when a sound reached his ears. It seemed to be the cry of a child. Peter maneuvered his horse to the alleyway but lost the sound. Retracing his steps, he secured his horse and went on foot.

He stopped, listened, and heard the sound again. Yes, he truly had heard the crying, it wasn't madness, he told himself. Peter picked his way through the streets, making note of the discarded items. A churn, a broken chair, several tubs, and empty casks were among the debris. It looked as though the owners had fled in haste without concern for their meager possessions.

Rounding the place where the butcher's shop had once known business, Peter spied the child. He was no more than seven or eight. Sprawled out across the body of a woman, the boy wept inconsolably and didn't even notice Peter until he was upon him.

"Son." Peter murmured the word, gently touching the boy's shoulder.

The child jumped to his feet in fear. He stood guard over the woman and refused to move, in spite of Peter's obvious interest in whether the woman lived or died.

"Is this your mother?" Peter questioned. "Is she sick?"

The boy's body jerked from sobbing, and his eyes were swollen from hours of crying.

"Son, I want to help you. I will not hurt her. I am a knight of the king, and I give you my pledge."

The boy seemed to take note of this. "She went to heaven," the child finally said and stepped back.

Peter saw no sign of blackened marks or swollen glands and wondered what had taken the young woman's life. "Was she sick for a long time?"

"No," the boy said, fighting back his tears and wiping his nose on his ragged sleeve. "She just fell down and never woke up."

"Was she your mother?" Peter asked gently, reaching out to touch the boy's shoulder again. This time he didn't resist.

"Aye," the boy said, before giving into his tears. "I want her to come back."

Peter felt strangely moved at the child's declaration. Had he not lost his own mother at an early age? He had never been allowed to give much thought to her passing, remembering his father's severity regarding Peter's childish tears. His father had been an advisor to the king, and he'd wanted no sissy for a child. Peter remembered a harsh reprimand and promise of punishment if he should so much as shed a single tear at her funeral mass.

Without thought to what he did, Peter scooped up the child into his arms and nestled the boy against his chest. The boy did not resist, but instead seemed to cling to Peter as though he were the last soul remaining on earth.

Peter had no idea how long he stood there. He stroked the boy's fine golden hair and spoke words he couldn't remember until the boy was finally sleeping and silent. What now? Peter wondered. What should he do with the child? He certainly couldn't leave him behind, and yet, where could he find help for him in the midst of the sickness? No one would have the time or inclination to care for a small boy such as this one.

Spying a wagon filled with straw, Peter gently placed the sleeping child there and went in search of a shovel. He planned to bury the woman before the child awoke, then perhaps he could decide what was to be done.

With each shovelful of dirt, Peter thought of the woman he buried and wondered by what means she had died. There was no mark upon her body or swollen bulges at the neck. Peter was by no means indiscreet enough to uncover her body and examine it in full. He had no medical training, and it seemed most indecent to even wonder at the matter. She was dead, and that was enough.

He finished tossing the last bit of dirt on the mound and then wondered at the lack of a priest to offer some service. Not knowing what else to do, Peter lifted his eyes heavenward and spoke. "Jehovah God, though I have not been a man who has spoken Your name oft', I have no other choice but to give this woman over to Your care. Have mercy on her soul."

When he looked down, Peter saw that the boy had joined him.

"Will God take care of my mother?" he asked soberly.

"Aye," Peter replied, uncertain whether he believed it or not. He smiled at the child. "What is your name?"

"Gideon," the boy replied.

"Well, Gideon, it looks like you will travel with me now. Have you anything to take along the journey?"

The boy shook his head but looked up with hopeful eyes. "You will not leave me here?"

"Nay, Gideon. I will not leave you." At the look of relief on the child's face, Peter suddenly knew that no matter the cost, he would not allow this child to be parted from him. Perhaps it was the fact he himself had been orphaned at an early age. Perhaps it was nothing more than honor and the vows of his knighthood. Whatever the cause might be, Peter knew his feelings were foreign to him, and while they troubled him deeply, they also provided a sense of strange comfort in a world gone mad.

"Come." He took the boy by the hand and led him back to where the horse stood. "We must ride hard if we are to keep the light of day. There is a place not far where we will seek shelter." Peter hoisted Gideon up with him onto the horse's back.

"I never rode a horse before," Gideon admitted.

"You will find it the very best way to travel," Peter answered with a smile.

Just as the sun dipped down below the horizon, Peter and Gideon arrived at the monastery. It seemed unnaturally quiet, and Peter presumed that it must be a time for prayers.

He lowered Gideon to the ground, dismounted, and rang the bell at the gate.

It wasn't long before a pale-faced monk appeared. He

shuffled forward, looking gaunt and sickly. "God be with thee, soul. What seekest thou?"

"A place to rest for the boy and myself. Perhaps a meal."

"This place is consumed with the fever," the man replied. "Ye cannot stay here."

"The plague has been our constant companion. Better to die here with the blessings of the good Lord, than to meet our fate upon the roadway, eh?"

The monk shrugged and opened the gate. "Ye have been warned, but so be the will of the Lord God. Enter and know peace."

Later, with Gideon nestled snugly against him, Peter thought back on the words of the monk. The man had spoken of the will of God. *What might that be?* Peter wondered. He had spent long hours in church, made vows in the name of the Lord, and pledged upon the relics of long dead saints, but these actions had been cause for little thought in his heart.

Gideon moaned in his sleep, and soon, little sobbing cries came in his restless slumber. Peter nudged the boy until he opened his watery eyes.

"'Tis only a bad dream," he told Gideon. "You are safe here."

"My mother is gone," Gideon replied sleepily.

"Aye," Peter replied. "But I am with you."

"You will not go?"

Peter smiled at the groggy boy. "Nay, I will not go."

four

Morning brought no hope. Peter, with Gideon ever at his side, found that most of the monks were consumed in various stages of the dreaded fever. The abbott himself lay near death, writhing and crying out in his misery.

"Have you food?" Peter asked the man who had admitted them the night before.

"There are stores of grain behind the bakehouse," the man replied. "If you seek a meal, I will show you the kitchen."

"Have all of your brothers fallen ill?" Peter questioned while they walked. He felt Gideon take hold of his hand, but said nothing. He squeezed the boy's fingers reassuringly and looked to the monk for an answer.

"Most have taken to their beds. Even now there are dead awaiting burial."

"Why is this?" Peter asked.

"No one has the strength to dig the graves," the monk replied sadly.

Peter nodded. "I will dig your graves. After we eat, you will show me what is to be done."

The monk seemed relieved at this declaration. "God has truly sent you. I will remember you in my prayers this day."

Digging graves became a consuming task. Peter toiled throughout the day, seeing no end in sight. The stench made him ill, but he forced his hands to continue turning the spadefuls of dirt. Gideon brought him water to drink, and when the sun appeared high overhead, a monk appeared with hard bread and cheese.

"The abbott has died," the man stated simply and turned

to walk away. He'd barely taken two steps when he collapsed to the ground.

Peter jumped up out of the hole and ran to the man. "He still lives, Gideon," he said, noting the anguish in the boy's eyes. Lifting the monk in his arms, Peter told Gideon to collect their food and go to the kitchen. "I will come there when I have seen this good man put to bed."

"You will not leave me?" Gideon asked, his voice quivering.

"Nay, Gideon. I gave you my word. I will not leave you."

Peter found two monks in the infirmary who had not yet succumbed to the fever. He delivered their dying brother to them with great remorse. "He has been good to me. I would know his name."

"He is Brother Francis," the man nearest Peter answered. "I am Brother Jude," he added.

"I am Peter. Sir Peter Donne, upon the king's business. I have been charged with assessing the extent of the fever and delivering into the hands of the abbott near York a package from His Majesty, King Edward."

"We are honored to share our humble home with you, sire," Brother Jude said somberly. "As you may well see, however, we are most compromised by this grave circumstance."

"Aye. I know it full well. I have this past morn buried many of your dead."

"Alas, we may but bless them and sew them into graveclothes," the monk said sadly. "'Tis no time for proper mass or tribute."

"Brother Francis had just told me of the abbott's death."

"Yea, but I fear we are too weak to even ring the bells. Surely God has turned His face, this day, from the sight of His children."

The days that followed passed much the same. Peter relieved his burial duties with short trips into the fields to hunt for meat. Gideon, ever fearful of desertion, watched Peter leave on these trips and would not touch a bit of food or even speak until his companion returned.

On the fourth day, Gideon awoke to a strange burning heat. He sat up in bed and realized that Peter still slept at his side. Reaching out a hand, Gideon found Peter hot to the touch.

"Peter," Gideon said, shaking the knight. "Peter, wake up."

The only sign of life came in the form of a moan. Gideon began to cry. "You said you would stay," he sobbed and fell against Peter's still form. "You said you would not go."

❧

"Push hard, Grace," Mary instructed. "The babe is nearly here." Mary knew the woman was exhausted. More than ten hours had passed since her labor had begun, and Mary feared for Grace's life and that of the child.

"I cannot do it, Mary," Grace panted, then let out a scream. "I cannot."

Mary silently contemplated the situation. There was naught that she could do, but let nature run its course. The babe's head was showing, but Grace had no energy to expel the child. She vaguely remembered her father speaking of a delivery where the woman had died, being too small to pass the child into life. He had then cut a larger opening and pulled the baby forth, allowing the child to live.

"Grace, you must listen to me. The babe cannot be born without your help."

Grace barely opened her eyes, and when she did, they were filled with pain. "Remember your promise Mary. Remember your promise."

"Grace, you will not die. I will not let you die!" Mary's voice rose anxiously. "I will get one of the men to help. They can push the child from on top, while you push from within."

Grace did not argue, and Mary took that as a sign of compliance. She saw that the men were congregated some twenty yards away, uneasy with the childbirth and Grace's screaming.

"James!" Mary called and moved across the open ground. "I need your assistance."

James separated from the group and met Mary halfway. "What be ye needin'?"

"You must help me with Grace. I need your strength to push the child out. Grace is not faring well, and I fear for her life and that of the babe."

James nodded and followed Mary to where Grace lay strangely still. "We be too late, mistress. She has already departed."

Mary looked down at Grace. "Nay!" she cried and threw herself down. "You cannot die, Grace."

"She is gone," the man said, crossing himself. "May God have mercy on her soul and on that of the wee one."

"Nay!" Mary reached into her father's bag and pulled out a knife. "I will not let it be so."

James stared in horror and fascination as Mary did what her father had once described and pulled the baby from Grace's body. For a moment, Mary feared she'd waited too long. The tiny baby girl lay blue and lifeless in Mary's hands. Quickly, Mary cleared the child's mouth and began vigorously rubbing the baby with a warm, wet cloth.

It started only as a tiny squeak, but then a mewing cry could be heard. Before long a lusty wail bellowed out from the baby, and Mary smiled satisfactorily at James. "She lives!"

"Yea, but the mother is no more. Mayhap it would have been better for the child to have stayed with her, for who will now care for it?"

"I will," Mary announced firmly. "I made Grace a promise."

"Yea, but the sickness is all around us. 'Twould be best for ye to leave the wee one here with its mother. Ye have no milk to give it nourishment and surely no nurse can be found upon the road."

"I made a promise to Grace. I will not break my vow."

James stepped forward and knelt down beside Mary and the baby. "The child will die—if not from hunger, then from the fever. The little ones are too weak to fight it." His soft words pierced her heart.

"I will find her food," Mary declared, wiping the eyes of the infant. "I will care for her, James. I must. I gave my word."

They buried Grace near the place where she'd died. James pounded a crudely formed cross upon her grave, while the other men placed stones upon the dirt to discourage interest from the wild animals of the region.

Mary stood to one side cuddling the baby. She had fed her a bit of honey-water, which seemed to satisfy the child for the time, but silently Mary wondered what she could do in the future. James had spoken correctly. The plague had a penchant for killing off the weak. And infant mortality itself held high numbers without the aid of epidemic sickness.

"Are ye ready?" James asked Mary softly.

"Aye, let us go." Mary reached down to pick up her father's bag, but James took it from her.

"Ye have the wee one to carry. I will take this for ye."

Just days before, Mary would have fought to the death anyone who would have tried to take her father's bag. The thought of even being parted momentarily from it had caused Mary to never allow it from her sight, but now things were different. The bag was, after all, not a living, breathing thing. It held precious memories and pieces of helpful, useful things, but it wasn't flesh and blood—unlike the child she cradled against her.

"Thank you," she whispered and followed James to where the others waited.

It was nearly dark when they spotted the monastery, and completely black when they approached the open gate. A single black cloth fluttered against the post, causing all but Mary to shy away. The baby now awoke, whimpered, and cried for food.

"'Tis the sickness," James announced, and the others nodded in agreement.

"I must find milk for the child," Mary said. She looked at the others who clearly would have no part of the monastery.

"We will travel on," James told her.

"Nay, I will stay here. Surely even a small monastery will have a goat or cow. I must feed the child."

"I will not risk my life on account of that baby," Edward stated. "I choose to go ahead."

"Aye," the others replied in unison.

"Very well, go. I chose to stay, and so we must part company here." Mary reached out and took her bag from James.

"God be with ye, Mary," James said softly. Even now the others were walking away from the gate. "I have come to care for ye. Are ye certain ye will not come ahead with us? You could leave the child here, for surely the monks will see to it."

Mary thought she'd misunderstood James's words. "Ye care for me?"

The darkness hid his face from her, but Mary heard the nervous cough he gave before continuing to speak. "I do. Will ye not leave the child and come north with us?"

Mary could scarce believe her ears. She'd never had a

man declare his interest in her, and it was a most disturbing moment for her. Finally, her senses returned and she realized that James had no interest in her keeping the baby.

"I made Grace a promise," Mary murmured. "I cannot go with you." Her voice sounded neither regretful nor sorrowful.

"I suppose I understand. A man's life is only as good as his word. A woman must feel likewise. Good life to ye, Mary," he said and was gone.

Mary stood for a moment longer before ringing the bell at the gate. When no one appeared to answer her call, Mary pushed the gate open wider and stepped into the yard.

A strange silence rose to meet her, not unlike that of deserted villages she had known on her trek with James and Grace. Were they all dead? Was no one left alive to help her?

She crossed the yard and went into the first building she came to. "Is anyone here?" she called out. Nothing.

Pressing forward, she passed from one room into another and realized herself to be in a small chapel. Candles surrounding a crucifix burned on the altar, illuminating the room in a haunting mixture of shadows and golden light. At least someone lived to light them, Mary reasoned.

The baby cried in misery, and Mary knew that her first goal must be to find nourishment for the child. Exiting the building, she hastily walked to the next and found it locked. Moving on, she finally entered what appeared to be the kitchen. Placing her bag on the table, Mary went in search of food for herself and the child. There was bread—hard with age but edible—and a pot containing some type of soup. The fire beneath it was barely kindled, so Mary placed the baby on the stone floor beside her and stoked the fire into a hearty blaze.

"Are you an angel?"

The voice so startled Mary that she grabbed the baby and jumped to her feet. Spying the small boy in the doorway, she let out a sigh.

"I am called Gideon. Are you an angel?"

"Nay," Mary replied. "I am Mary Beckett." The baby screamed out in misery and Mary tried to shush her with a crust of the ancient bread. "Suck on this, little one. 'Twill not help much, but I am looking for what will."

"Why is your baby crying?" Gideon asked.

"She is hungry, and I have no milk. Do you know if there is a goat or cow which might feed her?"

Gideon looked thoughtful for a moment, then his eyes grew wide. "I have a friend. His name is Peter, and he is very sick. If you come help him, I will find food for the baby."

Mary looked down doubtfully. "'Tis no game we play, Gideon. This child has scarce had a meal since her entry into the world."

"Please come. He promised he would never go away, but he is sick. Please. I will find food for the baby." Gideon's pleading was too much for Mary.

"Very well," she sighed. "Take me to your friend."

Mary took up her bag and followed the boy down a long, arched corridor. The unsettling silence clung to every stone, and Mary found herself almost wishing she had followed James.

"Help me. Help me."

The voice called from the room at Mary's right. "Wait Gideon," she called and stuck her head inside the room to see what the problem was.

It appeared to be an infirmary of sorts. Several beds were placed side by side, and in each one, a man lay in some stage of illness.

"Help me," the voice came again, and Mary went to the man who called out.

"What can I do for you?"

"Water, please," the man cried out. "Water, please."

Mary spied a bucket and ladle near the door. Placing the baby on an empty bed, she went to bring water to the man. Gideon frowned disapprovingly but said nothing.

"Are all of you ill with the fever?" Mary questioned.

"Aye. We are most nearly all dead." The man drank only a small amount, with most of that dribbling down his chin and onto his linen gown.

Mary thought to instruct Gideon to assist her, but the boy was gone. With a sigh, Mary felt the man's forehead and noted the swelling under his ears.

"'Tis the plague," she murmured to no one in particular. "Of that I am certain." There was nothing she could do but make them comfortable and watch them die. Hadn't she done as much in her own village?

Stoking up the fire and lighting several more candles, Mary wondered if there were others in the monastery who still lived. She turned to quiet the baby when Gideon appeared at the door, leading a small female goat.

The goat bleated in protest, but Gideon jerked the cord and came forward. "I found milk for the baby, now please come help Peter.

five

Mary sat Gideon in one corner and gave him the baby to hold. "I must milk the goat," she said. "You will sit here and hold her. She will most likely cry, but hold her close and do not drop her."

Gideon nodded at the awesome responsibility. Mary smiled at his sober face. "You are a good lad, Gideon."

Next, she took up the goat and after searching the kitchen for a bucket, tethered the nanny to a table leg and began to milk her. When enough milk covered the bottom of the bucket, Mary took it up and poured it into a small wooden bowl. She had no idea whatsoever how to actually get the milk into the baby. She rummaged in her father's bag but found nothing that would aid her.

Hearing the baby cry inconsolably, Mary took up a small piece of linen cloth from her bag and dipped it in the milk. She held it up and watched as the milk dripped from the cloth. It just might work. She took the bowl and cloth and went to where Gideon fussed and talked to the angry baby.

"Here," Mary said, putting the bowl down and taking up the baby. "Let's see if this works." She dipped the cloth again in the milk, then put it on the baby's lips.

The baby cried all the harder and milk oozed down her cheeks and neck. Mary, not to be outdone, took hold of the infant's face very gently and forced the cloth into her mouth. The baby began to suck and, to both Mary and Gideon's relief, instantly quieted. Mary repeated the process with the cloth until the baby had fallen asleep. With great satisfaction, Mary smiled at Gideon, and he smiled back.

"Now will you come take care of Peter?"

"Aye, Gideon. Take me to your friend."

"He didn't wake," Gideon said sorrowfully. "He has been sleeping for a long time."

Mary nodded and positioned Gideon in a corner on the floor and handed the sleeping baby to him. "Hold her carefully, like I showed you."

Gideon possessively took hold of the child. "I like her. What do you call her?"

Mary suddenly realized that the baby had no name. "I do not have a name for her yet. Would you like to think on one while I tend your friend?" Gideon nodded enthusiastically.

Mary picked up her bag and went to Peter's bedside. She wasn't prepared for what she found there. In spite of his illness, Peter's face had lost none of its rugged charm. His beard was a bit overgrown, which rather added to his appearance, but it was his long dark lashes against tanned, weathered cheeks that drew Mary's attention. She instantly wondered what color his eyes might be.

She sat down beside him and ran a finger lightly along his face. It was hot, as she knew it would be. She checked his neck for swelling and found none. A good sign, she told herself.

"Gideon, how many days has Peter had the fever?" she asked, looking over her shoulder.

Gideon shrugged. "I do not know."

"But you think it has been several days?"

"I went to sleep four times," Gideon answered.

"Four times? Did you wait for it to get dark or did you nap during the day as well?"

"No, I waited for the dark. I went with the monks. They showed me how to put the wet cloth on Peter's head."

Mary looked around and spied the bowl of water and cloth. "You must have done a good job, Gideon. Where are the monks now?"

Gideon shrugged again. "Most are sick, but there be some in the building by the well."

Mary felt a sense of relief. Perhaps others were still alive. Turning her attention back to Peter, Mary checked his breathing and heartbeat. If it had been at least four days since he'd fallen ill, then surely it wasn't the plague. Mary had seen time and again the dreaded swelling of the nodes, and blackened marks appeared by the third day.

"He is not sick like the others," she told Gideon. "I will watch him and care for him, but you will have to help me."

"I can help," Gideon assured her. "I will take care of Anne."

Mary looked at him. "Anne?"

"That is the name I picked for the baby."

"Why Anne?"

"My mother's name was Anne," the boy said, and his eyes filled with tears. "She lives in heaven with God."

"What of your father?" questioned Mary, reaching out to take the baby from the boy.

"He died afore I was born."

"I am most sincerely sorry for that. He would be proud of what a fine young man you've grown up to be," Mary said, putting a hand on Gideon's cheek. "Weep no more, Gideon. Anne and I have need of you."

"You will call her Anne?"

"Aye, it is a fine name for her," Mary replied. "Will you help me make her a bed?"

"I know the perfect bed for her," Gideon said, jumping to his feet. He ran from the room and was gone only a matter of minutes before he returned with an empty wooden box. "The monks used this for bringing in vegetables from the garden."

Mary smiled. "'Tis a perfect size. We must knock out the dirt and pad it with blankets."

"I can do it," Gideon said in an authoritative eight-year-old voice. He paused for a moment. "What are you called?"

"I am Mary."

"Like the mother of Jesus?"

Gideon's words surprised her. "I suppose 'tis true enough."

"My mother said Jesus came as a baby to the world. Do you think He was little like Anne?"

Mary did not know how to respond. She'd pushed aside thoughts of church and God for so very long. She had not been trained up in the way other children were. She knew various parts of church teaching, including the arrival of Christ to the world, but other knowledge was limited. "All babies," she finally said, "are born little."

Gideon nodded, satisfied with the answer. He went to work on Anne's little bed, leaving Mary in dumbfounded silence. *Why should it bother me?* Mary wondered. *I have lived these many years without concern about such matters. Father always said to place my trust in the real things of this world.* Mary looked down to the face of the sleeping baby. So tiny and frail, helplessly dependent upon someone bigger and stronger for the things of life. *Are we like that?* Mary wondered. *Be we frail beings who need an omnipotent God to watch over us? Or is it as Father said, we are creatures of our own making?*

Gideon soon returned with the box. It was prepared quite sufficiently. Even Mary agreed that she could not have done a better job. Gideon beamed with pride, while Anne slept contentedly in the vegetable box.

"I am going to see who else I might help," Mary told Gideon. "We will need to find supplies for the baby. Swaddling cloth to wrap her tightly so that she doesn't hurt herself by flailing her arms and legs and some other way to feed her."

"I can feed her like you showed me," Gideon reaffirmed.

"Aye, but there may yet be a better way. I will search it out. Will you stay here with Anne and Peter?" Mary questioned, glancing back at the form of the sleeping man.

"Aye," Gideon said, sitting down determinedly by the box. "I will watch over them, just like God watches over us."

Mary shook her head. "Why do say that Gideon?"

He looked at her with a genuinely puzzled expression. "Say what?"

"That God watches over us. Have the monks here taught you to say it or perhaps your mother before she died?"

Gideon still looked at her in surprise. "Aye, they say it too, but I know God is here."

Mary was intrigued. "How is this, Gideon?" She held her breath, awaiting the boy's response.

"Because He said He would be," Gideon replied without doubt. "In the Great Book, God said He would always be with us."

"The Great Book? You mean the collection of Scriptures the church uses?"

Gideon nodded enthusiastically. "I saw a bit of it. Brother Michael showed me. I cannot read the words, but my mother said that believing them was more important than just reading them."

"When did your mother tell you these things?" Mary could barely form the words. Gideon's faith filled her with a longing she could scarce understand.

Gideon's lips puckered a bit. "'Twas when the people were dying. She told me not to be afraid. We belong to God and He promised He would be with us." The little boy took great comfort in the words and repeated them. "He promised."

Mary felt a trembling within. She left the room without another word and hurried to the kitchen. What manner of child was Gideon that he should shake her beliefs to the very core of her reasoning? *He is but a boy with a childlike grasp of decades of church rhetoric. His words mean little in the face of those of a great man such as my father,* she reasoned. *He repeats what he finds comfort in. Nothing more.*

Going to the hearth, Mary sampled the soup that warmed there. The weak broth of rabbit gave Mary an insatiable appetite. She found another bowl and filled it with soup, managing to capture a few of the elusive pieces of meat.

Drinking it while she stood near the fire, Mary could not let go the words of Gideon's faith. "He promised He would be with us," the boy had said in complete devotion to a God he had never seen. A God who had taken his beloved mother and many others before his young eyes.

How can you love a God such as this? Mary wondered. She finished the soup and thought of taking up another portion. Perhaps there were those who were too ill to feed themselves, she thought. *Best I go about the place first, and see for myself if there are any to be cared for.*

In her search, Mary found seven dead monks and another dozen ill with the fever. Two of those who were sick seemed actually to be recovering from their ills. Mary saw to it that they had nourishment and promised to figure a way to remove them to a room away from the others.

Giving this new challenge some thought, she returned to find Gideon faithfully sleeping beside Anne. He had made a pallet of straw and blanket for himself upon the hard stone floor. Mary checked Peter and found him cooler, but still he slept undisturbed by her touch. *Who is this man?* she wondered. *What caused him to travel this way?* She sat beside him and lifted his hand in hers. It was a strong hand, calloused and large, with long slender fingers. Somehow it comforted her to hold it in her own for a moment.

"Wake up, Peter," she murmured against his fingers, not even realizing that she'd brought his hand to her lips. "Wake up that I might at least know the color of your eyes."

The man stirred, moaning an incoherent word. Mary dropped his hand as though she'd been caught doing something wrong. How foolish. She got up from the bed and tucked his arm at his side. She turned to check on Anne and only then did she notice that Gideon had prepared a pallet for her beside him. It was small, but she recognized it as a most welcome sight.

Seeing that she could do no more good for the night, Mary gratefully sought the refuge of the blanket and straw. With a sigh, she shivered and pulled the blanket closer.

Gideon rolled over and opened sleepy eyes for only a moment. "I said my prayers," he murmured, snuggling close, then fell back to sleep.

Mary looked at the sleeping boy for a long time. His peaceful face troubled her. In the face of horror and adversity, this small boy seemed confident of something she could not begin to reason for herself. This was not church litany or papal discourse. This was faith in its purest and simplest form.

six

Upon exploration, Mary found ten small rooms within the main building. Further investigation revealed a bake house, malt house, infirmary, dovecote, two chapels, and several storage buildings. And behind all of these were gardens, now desperately in need of care, and a great field left untended.

"Where are the people?" Mary asked one of the recovering monks. She knew that most monasteries were run just as castle lands. Instead of a great duke or earl, the abbott served as landlord to his tenants.

"Most are dead. The others have gone away in fear. When the abbott fell ill, they feared the curse of God was upon them and fled."

"And what do you believe, Brother James? Is the curse of God upon us?" Mary asked with intent interest.

The poor man seemed weary from just such contemplation. "I am of the mind that God allows His children to endure certain conflict for the purpose of strengthening and refining the good and destroying or redeeming the bad. Perhaps a great sickness is the only way in which God may attract the attention of some more stubborn souls."

"But if He be God, why should He stoop to the practices of man?"

The monk eyed her suspiciously. "Ye are not of a faith in His omniscience? Ye, a mere woman, would question the actions of God?"

Mary shrugged. "I daren't believe I deserve to be burned as a heretic, but blind obedience unto the church was not my father's way. I suppose now that he is dead, I am of an open mind for such matters. After all, my father's science did not keep him alive."

The monk nodded. "Nor could it. There is none save our God who has the ability to breathe life into flesh."

Mary thought on the words long after she'd left Brother James to sleep.

❧

Throughout the days that followed, Mary fell into an endless routine. Had it not been for Gideon, she would never have been able to accomplish much of anything. He proved to be quite capable at a number of tasks. He could milk the goat and feed the baby. He helped with the laundry of swaddling which Anne seemed quite happy to keep dirty for them, and always, he was devoted to Peter.

"Is he your kin?" Mary asked Gideon.

"Nay, he found me by my mother. He put her in the dirt and brought me here. He promised he would not leave me." Gideon spoke the words with a furtive glimpse at Peter's still form.

"Rather like God, eh, Gideon?"

Gideon smiled and nodded. "Aye."

"Yet Peter is silent and his sickness keeps him from reaching out to you. Is God silent too?" Surely it was unfair to expect an answer to such a question, but Mary posed it nonetheless.

"Sometimes God has to rest," Gideon said brightly. "I heard it said so. On the seventh day, God rested."

But there was no rest for Mary. She made litters to pull corpses to the graveyard and had no heart to mourn the passing of so many. Exhaustion became her constant companion, and fear and bitterness followed shortly behind. *If Ye be resting, God,* she thought silently, *then perhaps it is time You were awakened.* But instead, Mary felt something inside of her awaken—longing and desire to believe in something more than the death and dying around her. If only she could find the truth. If only she could know for sure whether God truly cared.

Toward the close of evening on the fourth day, Mary felt completely done in. She poured soup into a bowl, fully intending to eat it herself, then for a reason unbeknownst to her, she took up a spoon and went to the room where Peter lay sleeping.

Anne slept happily in her box, and Gideon was seeing to the chore of giving water to those who could still drink. Taking the soup, Mary sat beside Peter. Somehow she had known that he would open his eyes, and when he did, she found herself gazing deep into their warm brown depths.

"I have brought you broth," she said softly. "'Tis time you were up and about."

Peter smiled and tried in vain to reach up to touch Mary's face. "Be ye an angel?"

Mary laughed. "Gideon has already asked that question. Nay, I am no angel."

Peter closed his eyes as if contemplating her declaration. "Who are you?"

"I am Mary," she replied, then remembering Gideon's reaction to her name she hastened to add, "Mary Elizabeth Beckett."

"'Tis a beautiful name," he whispered hoarsely.

"Open your eyes, Peter," she said sternly. "You must take nourishment, and this broth will see you stronger."

Peter opened his eyes again. "How be it that you know my name?"

"Gideon told it to me." She placed the bowl upon the floor and propped Peter up as best she could. Retrieving the soup, she brought the spoon to Peter's lips. "Open," she commanded.

Peter allowed her to feed him without protest. By the time she'd given him most of the bowl, he seemed to have better color. His mind also seemed clearer, and he desired to talk.

"How came you here?" he questioned.

"I journey north to find my grandmother. I traveled with a band of pilgrims, and when I could not go on with them, they left me here at the monastery."

Peter suddenly seemed to remember the place. "I came here with Gideon. Where is the boy?" he asked, glancing about the room.

"He is helping me by giving water to the sick. I find I cannot be everywhere at once, and there are only two who seem to be recovering from the fever."

"The great fever?"

"Aye, the plague fever," Mary admitted. "Most of the brothers are dead, as well as the abbot."

Peter nodded. "I buried quite a few."

"I have replenished the supply," Mary commented. "I have not the strength to dig the graves, but the bodies are removed to help keep down the smell of the place."

Peter seemed all at once frightened. His eyes sought hers, and his breathing quickened. "Have I the fever?" he asked. Despair rang clear in his voice.

"Nay," Mary replied and instinctively reached out to put her hand against his bearded cheek. "Fear not. You have been ill with yet another cause. I am uncertain, but believe it to be nothing more serious than you have already known. I believe you will heal now."

Peter remained still against her touch. "How come ye by this knowledge?"

"I am a healer. My father was a doctor. He had trained at the university in Paris. I learned at his side, and though it is unacceptable for me to become a practicing physician, I am capable at my duties."

Peter nodded. "'Tis evident." His dark eyes held hers captive. "'Tis in your touch."

Realizing that her hand caressed Peter's face, Mary pulled away as though burned. She felt her face grow hot in embarrassment. Peter seemed not to notice, however, as he had closed his eyes. Mary thought perhaps he had gone to sleep and got up to leave.

"Please do not go," he called without opening his eyes. "'Tis most cowardly for a knight of the king, but I fear this time of sickness."

Mary stared down at his still form for a moment, then eased back down to the small space at his side. "'Tis not cowardly," she said softly.

Peter opened his eyes, and again, Mary noted the despair. "I fear, because I do not know the truth."

Mary felt her heart skip a beat. Had she not longed to know the truth, herself? Had she not pondered the reasoning of her faith, or lack of one, with this same desire in mind?

"The truth?" she questioned weakly.

Peter nodded. "I have known great wealth and power. I have served the king and been amply rewarded for my service. I have known many pleasures in this life, and yet, being here," he paused and glanced around the room, "they mean nothing."

Mary smiled. "I, too, have known comfort and possessions. My father kept me well before his death."

"And now you are alone?"

"I know naught," Mary replied softly. Her eyes welled with tears. Peter reached up and wiped at them as they ran down her cheeks. He nodded, understanding her pain.

"I know naught, either."

"Ye have no family?" she questioned, feeling uncomfortable with Peter's ministering.

"Nay, only God and king, and I am uncertain about God."

Mary nodded. "I suppose I can understand that well enough. Sickness causes a person to wonder upon his faith."

"Or lack of one," Peter added.

Mary trembled, for he had spoken her very heart into words. "'Tis fearful to face so much death and be uncertain," she finally allowed herself to say.

"Aye, Mary Elizabeth, 'tis most fearful. I have seen much death. Death upon the battlefields at Crecy. Death in the towns and villages where no soul remains to speak of the past. Too much death to ignore, yet I have no reasoning for such matters."

Mary smiled. "One of the monks suggested this is the only way in which God may attract the attention of more stubborn souls. Of this, I am certain to be one, but 'twould be more to my liking had God chosen another plan."

Peter tried to laugh but seemed to lack the strength. "I have been called worse than stubborn."

"That you are still here is proof enough of that," Mary teased.

"'Tis fear which keeps me here."

"How be this?"

Peter drew a heavy breath. "I fear dying without knowing God in truth. I have ignored much. Mayhap 'tis time I opened my eyes."

Mary nodded solemnly. "Perhaps you are right."

❧

The demands upon Mary continued. The sick grew sicker, and most died, leaving Mary to dispose of the bodies and work in desperation to keep down the stench. Those who were sick watched their comrades writhe in the tell-tell agony of painful terror. The system was affected in so many distinct ways that Mary could very nearly calculate the time of death for each person, well ahead of their appointment. First, the headache, weakness, and chills. Then the pulse became rapid, the speech slurred, and extreme fatigue sent the victim seeking the refuge of a bed. Of course, by that time the fever had gradually risen, and swelling of the nodes beneath the neck and in the groin were evident by the third day. From that point it was generally only another day or two at most. Mary knew that panic would strike each person. Her father said it was because the fever had literally baked the brain's ability to reason. What-ever the cause, people died in abject horror, smelling the smell of their own death, watching their flesh turn black with hemorrhaging blotches and festering wounds.

The real mystery came in those who actually recovered and in others still who died almost the same day they began to show symptoms of the illness. Mary could not hope to figure it out. All she could do was treat the ill as best she could and pray she did not succumb to the disease herself.

ॐ

Several days later, Peter gingerly swung his legs over the side of the bed and tested his strength by trying to stand. Gideon watched in silence, waiting to see if his dear friend would need his help.

Peter looked up with a sheepish smile. "At least I am on my feet."

Gideon nodded. "Mary will be pleased."

Peter's smile broadened. "You think it so?"

"Aye," Gideon said, coming to his side. "She is very kind."

"Aye, that she is," Peter said, remembering the black-haired beauty. Now that he was well on the road to recovery, Mary came less often to his room. She had even moved herself and Gideon to another room in order to afford Peter peace and quiet. The move had not met with his approval, but Peter had said nothing to stop her.

"She be pretty, too," Gideon said, pulling Peter from his thoughts.

"Has she vexed your heart, young sir?" Peter questioned, easing back down to the edge of the bed.

Gideon laughed. "I want to marry her. I think she is wonderful."

Peter looked at the boy with a stunned expression. "Gideon, you are too young for such thoughts."

"Then I will let you marry her. She needs someone to help her with the baby."

"Baby?"

"Baby Anne," Gideon said, as though Peter should already know this. "Mary let me name her." As if on cue, Anne began to cry from the room next door. "I have to go help her now," Gideon said and hurried out of the room.

Peter sat and stared at the open door for several moments. He had not known that Mary had a child. She had said nothing of it. In fact, she had told him she was alone. Or would be so if she found her grandmother to be dead.

He scratched the uncomfortable growth of beard. For sometime he'd worn his beard in the manner of Edward—a sort of homage. Then too, when he'd first grown it, Peter had thought it made him look more like a man than a boy. Now it just seemed cumbersome and irritating. Shaving, he decided, would be his first adventure for the day. He thought about asking Mary to assist him, but instantly discarded the thought. She was already working too hard. He'd seen her as she passed in the hall or when she'd come to check on his own progress. She had dark circles under her eyes. Beautiful eyes, Peter remembered, that were very near the shade of wild violets.

Anne's cries subsided and Peter wondered about the child. Was Mary's husband dead from the plague? She was far too beautiful to be left alone to wander the countryside, he decided. All manner of ill could befall her. He would speak to her later that night and suggest that she wait until he was back on his feet. *Then,* he thought, *I can provide her an escort and get to know her better.*

ᴥ

Mary startled at the sound of the abbey bell ringing. She hurried to the front gate and found a band of pilgrims. They were all filthy, some sick, and all starving. Two small children, wearing nothing but rags, peered out from behind their mother's swaying form. Mary blanched, for the woman already showed signs of swelling at the neck.

"We have the fever here," Mary announced, "but I see it is your companion as well. Come. I will tend you as best I can."

"We are humbly your servants," a man murmured before collapsing to the ground.

"Bring him," Mary said to two other men. She motioned the rest of the group to follow. "We have beds and some food. I will do what I can and take in return any help you feel strong enough to give."

Day blended into night, and Mary was not even sure where the hours had passed. Two pilgrims died within hours of their arrival. It seemed strange that they showed no signs of the plague, and Mary decided they must have died from sheer exhaustion and starvation. Three more with swelled nodes and fever-ridden bodies succumbed to the disease near dawn, and Mary could only add their bodies to the growing pile in the cemetery. It was a complete wonder that they had journeyed with the others. Sheer determination must have kept them on the road.

The mother with her two small children most worried Mary. She wanted very much for the woman to survive. She reminded Mary of Grace, and for that reason alone, Mary devoted herself to seeing the woman well. Two pairs of large, round eyes followed Mary's every move as she worked to ease the woman's suffering. The children were so tiny and frail that Mary worried perhaps they too were

sick. A cursory check of their bodies, however, relieved her
mind of such worries. Though they were dirty and ill-kept,
they showed no signs of illness.

Mary heard the cock crow and, with a hand to her aching
back, crossed the room wearily to look out the window. The
rosy pink dawn did little to lift her spirits. Another night of
death, she thought to herself. Another day of death.

The faint cry of Anne brought Mary to the realization that
she'd had very little to do with the baby since finding
Gideon such a willing helpmate. Checking the children and
their mother once more, Mary made her way down the hall.
I have to take care of Anne, she thought. *The baby needs me
now. Anne needs me.*

Mary kept pushing these thoughts through her head, hopeful that if she focused her attention on them, she could stay
awake and alert. Sleep pulled at her senses and dulled her
mind with dizziness. Reaching out to the stone wall, Mary
steadied herself for a moment before pushing on. She'd had
nothing to eat since the previous morning and little sleep
since she'd arrived at the monastery.

Anne's crying grew louder, and Mary fought hard to
make her legs work. She was so very tired. It seemed as
though she could not walk more than a step or two without
succumbing to her exhaustion. Leaning heavily against the
wall, Mary saw the room spin uncontrollably. *I cannot be
sick,* she thought. A sinking feeling of despair filled her heart.
*I cannot give in to this. Anne needs me. Gideon needs me.
Peter. . .*

She felt herself falling. "Peter," she whispered the name
as strong arms reached out to catch her.

"Mary!"

"You are here," she said weakly. "I simply said your name
and you appeared."

Peter's worried expression softened and a hint of a smile

played at his lips. "'Tis my lot, milady. Rescuing fair maids who have no one else to champion them." He lifted her easily into his arms. "You must rest now, Mary."

Mary nodded and allowed her head to fall back against his chest. How good it felt to rest. How good it felt to be held and cared for.

Mary was asleep before Peter could get her to a bed. He worried that she suffered from more than exhaustion, but seeing no sign of fever or swelling, he relaxed a bit.

She is beautiful, he thought, sweeping back ebony ringlets from her face. Her wild dark hair, tied simply at the nape of her neck, gave her a gypsy look. Peter could not tear himself away from her. Instead, he held her hand for a moment and wondered at the woman who had so selflessly cared for everyone else. Who was she? She dressed simply enough, but the cloak upon her bed revealed quality in its design, and the shoes upon her feet were nearly new.

The daughter of a physician, he remembered and wondered why she had introduced herself thusly, when she was obviously a wife or perhaps widow, and mother besides.

"Who are you, little Mary?" he whispered, before laying her hand gently across her waist. "And why have ye vexed me so sorely?"

seven

Peter used his new found strength to assist the monks in caring for their own. With Mary completely succumbed to exhaustion, Peter found filling her shoes an endless chore. He checked the abbey rooms for more dead and grimaced at the ever-present stench. When had he last breathed clean air? Air, sweet with the smell of wild flowers and new grass.

Coming upon the room where Mary had placed the woman and her children, Peter was greeted with the sobbing cries of the little ones. They couldn't be any older than two or three years, he surmised. Stepping closer, he found they had no fear of him but were simply mourning the loss of their mother.

"How is it," he murmured, closing the dead woman's eyes, "that ye know of her passing?"

The child who looked to be the oldest, crawled across his mother's body and touched Peter's hand. "Eat."

Peter smiled and lifted the child into arms. "So you are hungry." These words seemed to cause the other child to cry even harder. Scooping up the younger child, Peter carried them both to the kitchen and sat them on the floor.

"Play here, while I find you a bit of bread," he said softly.

Searching out the cupboards, Peter realized there was little food to feed the waifs. Mary had been the only one well enough to cook, and she certainly would have had little time to bake bread. Just as he feared there'd be nothing to satisfy their hungry, Peter happened upon a cupboard with several wheels of cheese.

"Ah, this will work nicely."

He tore two chunks and handed them to the children. With an appetite that stunned Peter, the children gobbled the cheese in moments and held up their hands for more. Hungry himself, Peter broke off several more pieces and picked up the children.

"We will go to where Gideon is," he told the two. "You will like Gideon. He is like you, only bigger. 'Tis of no matter though. Gideon has a big heart and will see you fed."

Peter went to the room where he'd left Mary sleeping soundly. He wanted to stay near her, yet worried that the noise would disturb her.

"'Tis little chance of that," he mused, and the children looked at him strangely. It would take a great deal of noise to penetrate Mary's exhaustion.

"Gideon," he called softly. There was no response.

Putting the children again on the floor, Peter handed them some cheese and went to search out Gideon. He remembered Mary saying that they'd taken the room next door, so Peter went there first and found Gideon feeding Anne.

"What have ye there, boy?" Peter questioned, seeing that Gideon held what looked to be a leather bag at Anne's tiny mouth.

"'Tis what Mary uses to feed Anne. She cut a tiny hole here," Gideon said, pulling the bag away from Anne.

Peter realized it was some type of coin purse. A single piece of leather had been folded in half and sewn up at the side, giving it a bit of squaring at the bottom. It was here where Mary had made the hole. As Anne began to fuss, Gideon popped the piece back into her mouth, and Peter had to laugh at the ingenious make-shift nipple.

"It works well," he said, ruffling Gideon's hair lightly. "I imagine some food in your belly would work well, too." Gideon nodded and Peter retrieved a chunk of cheese from inside his cotehardie.

"I cannot eat it and feed Anne."

"Mayhap, I could feed the babe," Peter said, uncertain even as he did so that this was a wise move on his part.

"Ye must hold her just like this," Gideon replied, evidently happy to be rid his burden. He pulled the bag away long enough for the exchange.

Peter sat rigidly on the bedside. Anne stared up at him with trusting blue eyes, wide and searching. She seemed mesmerized by Peter's face and for a moment forgot her lack of milk.

"Then ye hold the bag like this, else the milk will spill out," Gideon instructed.

Peter smiled when the baby latched onto the sack without further prompting. He held both just as Gideon had instructed. It was not the chore he'd feared. In fact, the baby stirred something deep within his heart.

"Will Mary die?" Gideon asked, taking Peter by surprise.

"I think not," he answered as evenly as possible. He prayed it would not be so.

"Good, I like her, and I do not wish for her to die." Gideon ate at his breakfast for a few moments before adding. "Will you marry her?"

Peter chuckled. "What a question! I know her naught, and she scarcely knows me. We both have our duties to see to and such a thing of marriage requires great consideration."

"I hope you will marry her," Gideon said with insistence. "Then you will be my father, and she will be my new mother."

Peter looked at the boy for a moment and said nothing. Gideon could not possibly know how his words affected Peter's heart. Peter was uncertain of their impact himself. Something in this waif and the others as well had caused him to consider all that was missing in his life. A wife and children had never been of interest to him. Living life one day to the next, answering only to his king, that was the life

Peter Donne had chosen. He'd stolen many a kiss and taken up many a bet, but always without commitment or concern for what the morrow would bring. Now, however, something had happened within him. Something different, deeper, and more personal than anything else he'd known.

Mortality was a frightful thing to consider. Especially one's own mortality. Peter had faced death and held it back at arm's length, but now, his own existence seemed worthless and frail. He had little to show for his exploits and no one to care.

"Can I see Mary?"

Gideon's voice brought Peter back to reality. "I think we will both go see her," he said, finding Anne asleep with little trickles of milk seeping out from the corners of her tiny lips. "Take this bag and do with it whatever you do. I will put Anne in her bed, and we will take her with us."

"The box is her bed," Gideon instructed.

Peter acknowledge his words by placing Anne gently in the wooden box. He smiled when she gave a satisfied sigh, fluttering her eyes open for a moment before closing them again in sleep.

Lifting the box, Peter told Gideon, "Bring your things. We will all stay in one room. That way we can keep an eye on Mary and you may help me with the other children."

"Others?" Gideon questioned.

"Two more," Peter replied. "Their mother died like yours. Will you be a brother to them so that they will not be afraid?"

Gideon's face lit up. "Aye and Anne will be their sister."

"That's a good boy."

Peter felt a sense of relief when he entered Mary's room and found the children sleeping soundly on the pile of straw Gideon had once used.

"What are they called?" Gideon asked.

"I know naught," Peter replied and placed Anne's box

near where they slept. "They are quite young. Mayhap we will have to name them."

"I named Anne," Gideon said with a smile of accomplishment.

"Mayhap you could think on two more names. I believe this one to be a boy child, but I do not know for certain. The other is a complete mystery, but I am certain given the needs of very small children, we will learn soon enough."

Gideon wrinkled his nose. "Babies make messes in their clothes."

Peter laughed out loud, then glanced at Mary, fearful he'd disturbed her sleep. "I must go about the abbey and see to fixing us something more substantial to eat. I must also see to the others. Will you be able to tend to all of this?"

Gideon's chest puffed up a bit as he threw back his shoulders. "I will take care of everyone."

"Thank you, sire," Peter said, giving a slight bow. "You will make a fine knight one day."

Peter hunted and killed two scrawny hares. They weren't much, he surmised, but they'd go well with the cabbage he'd located in the garden. He cleaned the animals and put them to boil with the cabbage in a huge black caldron before going to check on the sick.

Peter carried out the dead, nearly succumbing to the stench and losing his breakfast. Besides the children's mother, there were four additional monks who'd died in the night. Looking at the pile of bodies in various stages of decay, Peter could only imagine digging a very large hole and making a mass grave. There was no other way to handle the circumstance. There were simply too many bodies for him to dig individual graves for each one.

He set himself to the task and by late afternoon had managed to dig a good-sized pit. *'Tis not large enough,* he thought and decided to put off the burial until he could make it bigger. *What is one more day?* he reasoned.

Sweat soaked and dirt encrusted, he went to the kitchen and checked on the soup. The appetizing aroma wafted up to assail his senses. How very good it smelled. Peter thought that nothing he'd ever eaten tasted quite as good as this poor soup. After filling his bowl twice, Peter took down additional bowls and poured soup into each one. Hesitating, he ladled up one for Mary, uncertain as to whether she'd be able to eat.

Leaving these to cool, Peter took two more bowls to the recovering monks. Brother James and Brother Daniel were the only two men who seemed to be getting any stronger. Both were awake, but just barely able to sit, when Peter brought them the meal.

"'Tis poor fare," Peter told them with a smile. "I am not well trained in the kitchen."

The men smiled weakly and Brother James shrugged. "'Tis good simply to be able to partake. God's blessing on you for this meal."

Peter nodded and went back to the kitchen. He felt strange when reflecting upon the monk's blessing. Many had been the time when Peter had been blessed in pomp and ceremony, always dressed in elaborate fare, with hearty feasts and celebrations to follow. Such blessings seemed commonplace, almost insignificant. But Brother James's sincere blessing had been one of personal interest in Peter. God's blessing, he remembered thoughtfully. Lifting his eyes heavenward for just a moment, Peter contemplated just what that might entail.

Still deep in thought, Peter put the cooled soup on a tray and journeyed down the hall. Now he would check on Mary and the children. Something in his heart seemed to push him to hurry. A feeling of anticipation flooded his thoughts, and with a startling realization, Peter knew he looked forward to spending time with Mary and the children.

Gideon had the two new children preoccupied with a game he'd created out of counting straw. Anne slept peacefully, as did Mary, so Peter joined the children and offered them the soup.

"'Tis good," Gideon said. He took another long deep drink from the bowl and smiled. The other two children did the same and Peter noted that no sound of discontent came from either of them.

"Come and I will tell you a story," Peter said, beckoning the youngsters forward. They placed their empty bowls on the floor and scooted in closer while Peter began a tale of knightly bravery.

"On a great steed," he told them, "the king rode into battle."

"I rode on Peter's horse," Gideon told the little ones.

"Me ride," the boy said holding his arms out to Peter.

Peter laughed. "I will be your steed," he said and motioned Gideon. "Place him on my back, and I will ride him about the room."

Gideon thought this great fun and put the boy on Peter's back. Laughter bubbled up from the boy as Peter pranced about. It took only moments for the second child to insist on a turn. Peter obliged them both and even Gideon had a turn. They fell down laughing, Peter found himself attacked by the other two children, and soon a free-for-all of tickling and wrestling sent up peals of giggling to fill the room.

Mary awakened to the sound of laughter and thought how very good it seemed. For a moment she lay perfectly still, just taking it in and loving the very essence of it. Slowly, so as not to disturb the source, she rolled to her side and peered at the pile of wiggling bodies.

Peter Donne lay in the center of the pile, and Mary wanted to laugh out loud at the scene. Besides Gideon, the two children she'd seen with their mother were jumping up and down on the stately knight. Raising her head up on her elbow,

Mary couldn't prevent her hair from spilling down over the side of the bed. *What a fright I must look,* she thought, but put the matter away from her mind. The pleasure of the children's game was much more heartening to consider.

"It seems most every time I turn around," Mary said, bringing all eyes to her, "the number of children are doubling."

"Mary!" Gideon cried with a shout of pure joy. "You are not dead! Peter said you would not die."

Mary smiled at Gideon, then turned her gaze on Peter. His warm brown eyes met hers with an intensity that nearly caused her to look away.

"Is it well with you?" he questioned, shaking off children and getting to his feet.

"I feel much rested. How long have I slept?"

"Not nearly as long as you are going to," Peter said firmly. "I have some soup for you, but after that you must sleep some more. I fear our noise has disturbed that slumber."

"Nay," Mary said, sitting up. She started to get up, but Peter shook his head.

"I am quite serious, milady. You are to remain there for the rest of the day. I cannot see allowing you to cause yourself illness when there is little you can do, which I have not already seen to."

"But the children—" Mary started to protest.

"Are quite well. Anne sleeps and Gideon has shown me how to feed her. Gideon is quite capable of helping me with these little ones, so as you see, we are fine."

"But what of the sick?"

"Brother James and Brother Daniel are recovering nicely. The rest, I fear, will be dead within hours whether you tend them or not. I have done what I could, but they are too ill."

Mary nodded and fell back in resignation. Peter was right. There was little she could do. "What of the children's mother?"

"Dead," Peter said simply.

"I thought it would be so," Mary said softly. She lay in silence thinking back to her cursory examination of the woman. *I am so limited,* she thought. *There is so very little I can do and even Father's knowledge does not enable me to save them.* She looked thoughtfully at the children, realizing that she would somehow have to care for two more. With a smile she met Gideon's enthusiastic face and questioned Peter. "How came you by Gideon? He says you found him."

Peter brought the soup and sat down beside Mary. Already Gideon and the other two children were playing. "Here, sit up and drink this. 'Tis soup I made, and though weak, 'tis better than nothing."

Mary again sat up and rested against the stone wall. She tasted the broth and smiled. "'Tis quite good. You shame yourself by calling it weak. 'Tis most hearty."

Peter chuckled. "I thought it quite good, myself. When one is hungry, truly hungry, even a crust of bread seems like a feast."

"So tell me of Gideon," Mary said between sips of soup.

"'Tis naught much to tell. I found him weeping over his dead mother, much the same as these young waifs. I knew I could not leave him." Peter stared hard at Mary, causing her heart to skip a beat. "I brought him here, and surely you must know the rest better than I."

"I had scarce stepped foot through the gate when Gideon greeted us and pleaded for me to see to his friend. A more devoted ally surely could never be found."

Peter smiled. "I cannot say why, but I feel obligated to the child."

"He said you would get well, for you had promised to never leave him." Mary could only wonder what such a commitment by Peter might mean to her. Something about him caused her heart to flutter wildly, and the nearness of him made her feel safe and cared for.

"Aye, I promised, and I am a man of my word."

Mary met his eyes hesitantly. She started to speak, but just then Anne began to fuss.

"I will feed her," Gideon said authoritatively. "I must go get milk." He took up the bag and went off in search of the goat.

"Why is it that you do not feed her?" Peter questioned off-handedly.

Mary nearly laughed out loud at the expression which crossed Peter's flushed face when he realized how personal the question was. "Anne is not my child," Mary offered simply. "I helped her into the world, but her mother died. The folk I traveled with would have me leave her to die as well. I chose motherhood over murder."

Peter nodded. "And I chose fatherhood over desertion."

Mary laughed. "What of the other two? Shall we split them?" She asked in jest but saw Peter's face grow sober.

"'Twould seem unfair—they have come together."

Mary nodded. "'Twas not a serious question, Peter. I would never dream of separating them. They are a family."

"A family," Peter murmured. "'Tis a good word."

"Aye," Mary said, feeling her breath catch in her throat. She looked across the room to the two children as they played with the fussing baby. Without thought, she looked back to Peter, whose eyes seemed to reflect all that she was feeling.

"We will not separate them," Peter said firmly.

"Nay," Mary affirmed. "We will not."

eight

The silent empty halls of the monastery bore no evidence of the peaceful worship that had at one time been resident. Mary drifted through the hallowed chapel, now untended and forgotten like the guests of a wedding once the bride and groom have gone. She counted the days to be nearly twenty since her arrival. By those calculations, Anne was nearly a month old and soon the weather would turn cold and make traveling difficult.

"I thought you were resting," Peter said from the door of the chapel.

"I am," Mary said with a smile.

"The little ones are napping, and you ought to be as well," Peter said, with a slight reprimanding tone to his words.

Mary stared at Peter for a moment and realized that he brought something alive in her. Something that she'd never known in all her years. His gaze met hers and it seemed to Mary that he could read her thoughts, for his eyes blazed passionately, causing her to tremble.

He stepped forward, and Mary noted his legs beneath the tight-fitting hose were heavily muscled and firm. He wasn't a tall man, no more so than average, she thought, but he carried himself with the air of one acquainted with nobility.

When he stopped only a few paces from her, Mary allowed her eyes to travel up to meet his face. He smiled rather roguishly, causing her to blush.

"You examine me with a physician's eye," he teased.

"Hardly that," Mary said, without thinking. Peter laughed heartily at this, causing her blush to deepen. "I only meant that. . ." She fell silent. How could she explain to him that she had yet to ever feel such heartfelt stirring when contemplating a mere patient?

"You only meant what?" Peter questioned softly.

Mary shook her head. "Mayhap later," she said with a hint of a smile. "Now seems not the time or place."

Peter reached out and took hold of her hand. "Then let us walk and pass both the time and the place. I would know what is in your thoughts, sweet Mary."

Mary allowed him to lead her, but only because his comment had taken her by surprise. *Sweet Mary?* she wondered. *He says my name with such an endearment and acts as though nothing is amiss.*

"Did you hear me?"

Mary jerked up her head, almost afraid to meet his seeking eyes. "I admit I did not."

Peter grinned and opened the door. Passing through, Mary found them to be in the unkempt garden grounds. She realized immediately that Peter intended to continue their conversation when he led her to a small bench and motioned her to sit.

"Now that I might have your attention," he said lightly, "I asked what plans you had for the future."

"Oh," Mary replied, hoping she didn't sound disappointed. "I suppose I have not thought much on it. My goal is still to journey north and seek out my grandmother. However, I felt it only right that I remain to help with the dying and encourage the healing in others."

Peter nodded. "Brother James and Brother Daniel are the only ones left. The abbey is desperately neglected, but what else can they do? There is no one to reap the grain, much less to collect the rents and oversee the land—that is if there were those left to rent and work the lands."

"'Tis sad to see the devastation. I am tired of death and

yet there is no place where it seems not to be." Her voice sounded sad, even in her own ears, so it didn't surprise her when Peter put his hand upon hers. It was a bold move, but the times were such that many proprieties were cast aside for the comfort one might seek.

"Mayhap in the north we will find there is less sickness," he offered softly.

"We?" Mary questioned, unable to keep her voice from revealing the surprise she felt.

"I am about the King's work," Peter answered with a shrug. "My business takes me north, and there is no reason we should not journey together."

Mary relaxed a bit. In her heart she thrilled to this announcement. She knew the journey would be a taxing one with the children, yet it was the separation from Peter that troubled her more than she was ready to admit.

"Brother James has given me a donkey and cart," Mary finally said. "He thought it would be easier to travel with the children that way."

"Aye, he told me this morning. There will also be provisions, for he showed me where to find the foods in storage. 'Twill make the journey much easier, as well."

The silence fell awkwardly between them, and Mary wished she could tell Peter what thoughts were on her heart. But how could she explain them? She scarcely understood them herself. He haunted her every thought, and when she closed her eyes in sleep, it was his face which met her in her dreams.

"We should begin before much longer," Peter told her.

"'Tis certain we cannot wait or it will turn rainy and be too hard on the children."

"Aye," Peter agreed. "I propose we start on the morrow. What say you to this?"

"Very well," Mary replied, then thought of a matter which

had caused her much consideration. "Peter," she began slowly, "what of Gideon? I have a great fondness for him, and he is very helpful to me with the children. I know you have promised to never leave him, but as a knight of the King, can you, in all truth, keep that promise?"

Peter studied her for a moment before answering. "I, too, am quite fond of the boy. He has become a son to me in every aspect. The other little ones, as well, are important and have managed to secure a place here," he said with a hand to his chest. "I have given some thought to the matter, however. Your words are true enough, and it would be unfair to drag the boy to the battlefields, at least not without proper training."

Just then Gideon interrupted them. "Peter! Brother James sent me to fetch you."

Peter glanced from Mary to where Gideon stood in the stone archway. "I will come," he stated, then getting to his feet, offered Mary his hand.

Mary took it hesitantly, knowing the effect of his touch on her being. Refusing to meet his gaze, Mary looked to where Gideon danced around the arch, waiting for Peter.

"Then you do agree to our accompanying you and the children?" Peter questioned, moving toward the archway.

"I am very happy for the protection and companionship," Mary replied. "I am also glad that I may postpone bidding farewell to Gideon."

Peter tightened his hold for a moment, then paused. Mary looked up, wondering why he had stopped. Peter searched her face. Mary shifted uneasily. *What is he looking for?* she wondered. *Have I not offered my approval?*

When Mary blushed under his scrutiny, Peter grinned. "I am glad, too. For I am delighted at the prospects of postponing my farewell to you, sweet Mary." He lifted her hand, kissed it lightly, then left her to join Gideon.

As he walked away, Mary's face broke into a smile. *He must have feelings for me,* as well, she mused. Her smile broadened, and she was glad that Peter had his back to her. She did not notice Gideon's watchful eye, however.

In the kitchen, Mary sampled a thick mutton stew and smiled. It reminded her of days gone by with her father. It surprised her that she'd thought so little of him in the last weeks. True, the work had been merciless in its demands, but her father had been more dear to her than life itself.

"You always loved my stew," she said softly and tasted another spoonful. "You said it stuck to your ribs, and I teased you that your knowledge of anatomy had gone sour." Mary cherished the memory.

Crossing the room, she put bowls on the trestle table and pulled up a long bench which Peter had brought from elsewhere. It worked well to feed the children here, and Mary was grateful for such simplicity. Her final chore while the stew simmered was to milk the goats. Brother James had advised her where others were to be found, and once Mary and Peter understood the extent and needs of the livestock, they became the keepers of the same. There were eight goats, three of which were nursing nannies who always seemed to have plenty of milk to share. Mary happily accepted this, as the other two children were small enough to crave milk, just as Anne did. Gideon had named the boy William, and his younger sister was to be called Sarah. Mary thought them perfect names, and even William and Sarah accepted the change without objection.

"So long as their bellies are filled," Mary said to herself, "it matters little what they are called."

"Who are you talking to?" Gideon asked, stepping into the room and looking around.

Mary startled but recovered her composure. "I was simply thinking aloud, Master Gideon. 'Tis time I milk the goats."

"I can milk them for you," Gideon offered.

"Mayhap we should milk them together," Mary countered. "It will make the work half for each of us."

Gideon agreed to the arrangement and followed Mary into the yard. The small stone building which housed the animals doubled as stables and smithshop. The goats instantly began bleating at the appearance of Mary and Gideon.

"We have become good friends, no?" Mary suggested.

"Aye, this one is my favorite," Gideon said, pointing to the black and white nanny who searched his hand for a treat.

Taking up stools and buckets, Mary and Gideon went to their task in silence. The sound of milk being squeezed out into the wooden buckets made rhythmic music against the stillness. *'Tis comforting,* Mary thought with a sigh of contentment. *These simple tasks and the companionship of a child are more to me than I had imagined them.*

"I saw you smile like that at Peter this morn," Gideon said, startling Mary.

Peter was just passing by when he heard Gideon's comment to Mary. Standing still against the stone frame, he waited to hear what response Mary might give the boy.

"What nonsense are you speaking now, Gideon?" Mary questioned.

"I saw you smile after Peter kissed your hand. Do you love Peter?"

Peter wanted to chuckle at the child's brazen question, but he also wanted to hear Mary's answer. He had seen something in her eyes that gave him reason to believe her feelings for him were every bit as strong as his for her. However, every time they had a moment in which to speak of it, Mary would either change the subject or someone would interrupt them. Peter intended that no one interrupt Mary's reply to the boy.

"What a question!" He heard her say. "I cannot say when

I have ever known a child as presumptuous as you."

"What is presum, presum—"

"Presumptuous," Mary filled in. "'Tis a word which means you asked a very personal question which deserves no answer because," she paused and Peter wondered what she would say. "Because. . .because 'tis none of your concern."

"But it is," Gideon protested. "Peter is going to be my new father, and I told him that I wanted him to marry you so that you could be my new mother and Anne could be my sister. Now William and Sarah can be in our family too."

"Gideon!" This time, Peter did laugh softly at the shocked tone Mary's voice held.

"You always look at him different like," Gideon said. "And when you smiled this morn, you looked so happy. I think you love him, and I am glad."

"Gideon, stop this minute. Whether I do or not is nothing for me to speak on with you."

Peter was completely intrigued by the conversation. She hadn't once denied the possibility, nor indicated an unwillingness to such a matter. Could it be possible she loved him, just as he almost certainly loved her?

"Will you speak to Peter on it?"

Peter heard Gideon voice the question and again nearly laughed out loud. *Good boy,* he thought. *Make it clear that she needs to bring it to me.*

"Nay!" Mary replied in a voice that betrayed her concern. "I will not, and neither will you. Peter has enough to think on, and we will not vex him with such matters."

Peter heard rustling sounds and knew that Mary and Gideon had completed their milking. He moved quietly in the direction of the kitchen, whistling to himself as he did so. *She must have feelings for me,* he decided. *Otherwise she would not have hesitated to deny them to the boy.* His whistling stopped as a smiled drew up the corners of his lips. *Ah, sweet Mary,* he thought and felt his heart pound a little harder. *You already vex me with such matters.*

He paused at the door and turned to see Mary and Gideon head up the walk. Gideon struggled with his bucket, and Mary leaned over to retrieve it.

"Might I offer a hand?" Peter questioned, coming toward them as though he were heading out instead of coming in.

Mary blushed and quickly lowered her face. "Not a word, Gideon," Peter heard her whisper.

"Telling secrets, Mary?" Peter questioned, taking the buckets.

Mary looked up and met his stare. "I. . .we were just. . ." She squared her shoulders and brushed past him. "I have to tend the stew."

Peter laughed and followed with the buckets, while Gideon fairly danced through the open door. He was going to enjoy drawing this secret out of Mary's heart.

nine

Mary smiled back at Gideon with a strong sense of satisfaction. The small, two-wheeled cart made a perfect traveling coach for the children, while Mary found her ease—what little could be had—on the roughly hewn driver's seat. The donkey, a beefy little character with a surprisingly good nature, seemed unburdened by the chore of pulling them. The children were excited and perceived the journey with imaginative enthusiasm. The goat, their new traveling companion, did not think much of his new circumstance. It made Mary chuckle.

"'Tis better to watch the road before you," Peter said, riding up beside her.

Mary turned back to check the road before lifting violet eyes to meet his glance. She could think of nothing witty to reply and so simply met his gaze and returned her attention to the donkey.

What is it about him? Mary pondered. *Since the first moment he opened his feverish eyes, I have found myself most captivated.* The thought that Peter had somehow captured her wakeful attentions, as well as her nighttime dreams, truly vexed Mary. *Is this love?* she wondered.

"And where do your thoughts lead you today, Mary?"

Peter's voice caused Mary to tighten her hands on the reins.

"To the future, sire," she answered honestly. Let him make of it what he would, she mused.

"Ah, yes," Peter murmured from above her. Mary refused to look at him again, so Peter continued. "Have you given more thought to these babes and how you will care for them?"

Mary shook her head. "Nay, 'tis a heavy matter for certain. I can only pray my grandmother is still alive and that she is still a wealthy woman."

"And if she is not?"

"Why do you ask me these things?" Mary questioned more harshly than she'd intended. "You know full well that I have naught to offer them. I am alone in this world. Why cause me to continuously ponder the matter?"

"Mayhap because the matter will not ponder itself." His words were gently offered. "I have considered it myself, and it is not a problem easily resolved. Children need food, clothing, warmth, and love. I have little doubt that you can offer them love, but what of anything else? By your own admission you have no home. Therefore, they have no home so long as they live with you."

Mary nodded without looking up. "I know it well."

"I say not these thing to grieve thee, Mary. 'Tis simply something to be considered with a clear mind. Out here, away from the crowds and the dying, it seems best to regard these matters at length."

"I will think on them by and by," Mary offered and said nothing more.

Peter scouted the areas alongside the road, all the while keeping the little cart within view. _She is wonderful_, he thought, allowing himself a brief glimpse of Mary. The wind picked up enough to play havoc with her long dark curls. She had tied them at the nape of her neck and Peter was captivated by the way they rolled down her back in blackened waves. Were she a lady of court or of more noble means, no doubt her hair would have been braided and bound, hidden away beneath any number of coverings. He tried to imagine her in the jewel-encrusted robes favored by the queen or in the rich velvet surcoats trimmed in fur which had been so popular amidst the ladies at court.

Peter shook off the image of finery, however, and concentrated on the woman he saw. She wore a simple surcoat and linen tunic, and Peter thought her more beautiful than all the noble ladies of London.

Just then a noise to his left, caught Peter's attention. It sounded like the cries of a child. He reined back on his horse and strained to listen. It was distant but nevertheless very real. Peter waited for Mary to catch up to him before swinging down from his mount and throwing the reins to her.

"I heard a cry. Hold the beast while I go search it out." Peter didn't wait for her approval before taking off in the direction of the cry. Gnarled limbs and briar branches made his passage into the woods difficult. Overhead, huge oaks sheltered the forest floor from the pale yellow light of the sun. The deeper into the woods he went, the darker it grew. Only the moaning sobs kept him pushing forward.

Except for the cries, an eerie silence gripped the forest. It seemed unnatural to Peter, yet was not most of the world in an unnatural state?

Catching his pointed-toed boot against a tangle of vines, Peter nearly fell headlong onto the ground. Righting himself, he paused long enough to determine the direction of the crying before pushing on.

Just as he began to fear he would never locate the source of the cries, Peter found himself standing before a young girl. She was scarcely more than a mite, so tiny and frail, yet Peter judged her to be Gideon's age. She looked up at the stout knight with huge, fearful eyes, and Peter's heart melted.

"Are ye hurt?"

She nodded, but said nothing. Tears still poured down her face, but the sobbing had ceased.

Peter knelt beside her, but the child push back and cried out in pain. "Do not fear me," he said, putting a hand out to still her. "I have come to help. Where are you hurt?"

"I fell," she whimpered. "I hurt my leg."

Peter gently lifted back the loose linen of her skirt. The leg in question was swollen and purple just below the child's left knee. "I have a friend with me," he told the girl. "She is a great healer. We will have her look at this." The child still eyed him fearfully. "What is your name?" Peter asked her.

"Gwenny," the girl replied.

"And where be your parents?"

"I do not know. We ran when the bad people came to our house. I got lost, and I could not find my mama."

"How old are you, Gwenny?"

"Almost ten years," she answered, seeming quite proud of this.

Surprise flickered across Peter's face. Such a tiny thing, he thought and reached out to lift her. "I am Peter. I will carry you to our wagon. Mary, the woman I spoke of, will tend to your leg." The girl did not resist Peter, and so he continued talking as he walked. "We have other children with us as well. Their parents are dead, however. You are welcome to stay with us. We are going north, and mayhap we will find your people."

Peter emerged from the woods to find Mary restlessly pacing the road. She had tied off the donkey and horse to allow them to graze, and waited most impatiently for his return. Peter saw her expression soften the minute she spied his baggage.

"Is she hurt?" Mary questioned.

"Aye, her leg is broken," Peter replied, and the child looked up at him fearfully.

"Will ye cut it off?" she questioned, nearly hysterical.

"Nay," Mary soothed, reaching out to push back matted

brown hair from the girl's face. "Do not be afraid. I will look at your leg, and we will figure how to best treat it."

"Her name is Gwenny," Peter said, taking the child to a grassy spot where Mary already knelt in anticipation of the examination.

"And how old are you, Gwenny?" Mary asked, lifting the child's skirt to observe the leg.

"Ten years," the child replied again to the question Peter had already asked.

Peter watched Mary's gentle ministering. She felt the leg tenderly, talking all the while to the frightened child. When at last she was satisfied with her examination, she bade Gwenny to remain still, while she and Peter gathered the things they would need to help her.

Mary motioned Peter away from the child. "'Tis broken, but I believe we can set it to better heal."

"What can I do?"

"I will need two sturdy sticks. At least as thick as Gideon's arm." Peter nodded. "We will have to pull the leg back into place. Father said a broken bone must always be pulled apart first, then be allowed to go back together. I have not set one by myself, but I have watched it done. I will need your strength to hold the girl while I pull the leg."

"I understand. Let me find your sticks. Do you need anything else?"

"Nay, I have some herbs which will help with the pain, and I will tear strips of cloth from my kirtle to bind the leg." Even as she spoke, Mary lifted her surcoat and ripped a portion of the under cloth away.

Peter noted shapely ankles before the surcoat was dropped back into place. "I will get the wood."

He returned quickly and noted that the children were already stirring in the cart. "You must be very quiet," he told the three oldest. "This little girl has a broken leg, and Mary is going to fix it." Gideon nodded in somber silence, while William and Sarah just stared in curiosity.

"Will these do?" Peter questioned, and Mary reached up to examine the two sticks.

"They are perfect. Can you trim off the ragged points?"

"Certainly, milady." Peter did as she asked and returned the smoothed sticks.

"Peter will hold your arms, Gwenny. Remember, I told you it would hurt a bit while we pull on your leg, but then I will bind it up and it will not hurt as much."

Gwenny nodded, fear written clearly in her eyes. Peter patted her gently on the head and took up a position behind her. He waited for Mary's direction, fascinated as she nimbly worked with her meager supplies.

She gave Gwenny a piece of twisted cloth. "Bite on this—'twill ease the pain."

The child took the cloth hesitantly, and Mary nodded to Peter. Gently, Peter gripped the child around the arms and pulled her back against him. "'Twill be like a big hug," he whispered in her ear. "Just pretend I am a bear." This made the girl giggle.

"I will pull on the count of two," Mary told Gwenny. She looked to Peter and added. "You must hold her firm until I say otherwise."

"I will do just as you bid, milady." Peter hoped that Mary saw the tenderness he felt for her. She seemed so strained by the task, almost as though she felt every bit of the child's pain.

"Very well. One. Two." Mary pulled and Peter held the screaming child tight. He actually heard the bone snap into place. Mary released her hold, admonishing Gwenny not to move. It was an unnecessary directive, however, as the child had already fainted from the pain. This only made Mary's task easier, and she smiled up at Peter when she saw him stroking the child's forehead.

"'Twould seem we have added to our family," she quipped.

Peter started at the suggestion. They truly had become a family, and he liked it very much. How could he just allow Mary and the children to wander out of his life? Even this child seemed precious to his heart. What had become of the fun-loving rogue of his younger years?

"'Tis set," Mary exclaimed, tying the final piece of cloth in place.

"I'll make her a place in the cart," Peter said, gently easing the child onto the ground. "Will she heal?"

"I believe so," Mary replied. "The break is clean; it did not cut through the skin, and that is good. She is young and seemingly strong, and that, too, is good.

Peter nodded and looked to the wagon where three sets of eyes peered down at him and Mary. "'Twould seem we have an audience," he whispered and got to his feet. "We will need a soft place for her to rest," Peter said, coming to the cart. "Gideon, smooth out the straw over there, and I will bring her."

Gideon immediately went to the task, just as Anne began to fret and cry. Mary went to Anne, and Peter gently carried Gwenny to the wagon. Placing her in the cart, Peter motioned Gideon to bring Mary's mantle.

"Will you watch over her, Gideon?" Peter questioned man to man. "'Tis the responsibility of men to care for the women. Gwenny is older than you, but she is more frail and in need of your care. Can you do this thing for Mary and for me?"

Gideon's countenance glowed with pride. "I will care for her, Peter. I will do a good job. You will see."

"I knew I could count on you, Gideon. You will make a fine knight one day."

Their journey north continued, and before they had been gone from the monastery even a week, heavy rains made their labors nearly impossible. More than once they stopped for the night in a nearly deserted town, only to be faced once again with the despair and heartache that accompanied the plague.

Mary did what she could for those who remained behind, but for the most part, people were superstitious and wanted no part of strangers. The most troubling sight to Mary was the deserted children. Some were orphaned by the death of their parents, while others were deserted and left to die because of superstitious nonsense and rhetoric.

"Do you know," Mary said in a voice bordering on rage, "that this baby was left to die because the parents were convinced he had caused the sickness in the village?"

Peter looked down at the infant in Mary's arms. No more than a year old, the chubby boy reached out for a lock of Mary's hair.

"Pray tell, why would they consider such a matter valid?" Peter questioned, taking the child from Mary's trembling arms.

"Because he bears a mark upon his back," she said, with clenched fists at her side. "I cannot believe such superstition would allow a mother to leave her child. This baby is barely walking and certainly could not have been weaned. How could she leave him, Peter?"

Mary knew her temper was out of control, but it no longer mattered. This child was innocent of wrong-doing, yet an entire village marked him as the cause of their woes, simply because he bore a mark which made him different. Tears came to her eyes as she watched the roly-poly baby giggle with glee, while Peter made growling noises against the baby's stomach.

It was simply too much to bear. How could there be so

much cruelty and stupidity? Unable to stave back the tears, Mary stalked off to a place away from the wagon and the other children. She did not wish them to see her break down.

"Oh, Papa," she moaned, remembering her father's gentle touch and kindness to her when she'd been sad. How she longed for his embrace and tender words of love. He had been her entire life, and now he was gone. Somehow in the face of such ruthlessness the pain seemed worse than it had before.

Leaning against a towering oak, Mary hugged her arms to her breast. It could not fill the emptiness inside. *Why do You allow such pain, God?* she wondered silently. *If You are truly merciful and all-knowing as the good monks told me, why do You hurt Your children so?*

"Mary?"

She turned her reddened eyes to Peter's gentle voice.

"People are ignorant," he said softly. "They do what they believe they must and know not why such things should be perceived as strange. There must be hope, though. We are here, and we will care for the babe."

"But what of all the others?" Mary questioned. "There must be many more who have been left behind because of nonsense such as markings or superstitious mumblings. Surely even God is not so cruel."

"Nay, I do not believe God to be cruel," Peter said, lifting her chin. "We must have hope, sweet Mary. Surely God Himself has led us to these little ones. Think on that. There is only so much we can do. Only so many we can care for."

Mary felt her heart skip a beat at the loving expression on Peter's face. Without thought, she reached her hand up to touch his cheek. The bristle of his newly-formed beard felt foreign, but Mary loved the feel of it and ran her thumb across his jawline.

She heard Peter's quick intake of breath before his hand

closed over her wrist and pulled her hand away. "Come sit with me," he said, pulling her along.

"But, the children. . ."

"Gideon has it all under control, and Gwenny is feeding Anne."

Mary felt her raw emotions and wondered with fear if she had somehow offended Peter with her touch. Immediately she sought to apologize as Peter pulled her deeper into the cover of the forest.

"I am sorry for my boldness," she whispered.

"I am not," Peter replied and swept her into arms.

Mary felt her breath catch as Peter's lips touched gently hers. The kiss left her breathless and without warning, she crumbled to her knees when Peter released her.

"Mary!" Peter exclaimed, kneeling beside her.

Dark hair tumbled over her shoulder, hiding her face. For once, Mary was glad for her disheveled state. She desired nothing more than to hide her face from Peter. What a wondrous but confusing feeling she held in her heart. How could she dare to face him and try to explain?

"Mary?" he said again, this time much calmer. He turned her face, forcing her to look at him. "Are ye well?"

Mary nodded, her eyes huge in wonderment. "I am."

Peter grinned and Mary felt her face grow hot at his words. "'Tis your first kiss, am I right?"

"'Tis no concern of yours, sire," Mary said, pushing his hand away. She was completely humiliated for reasons beyond her understanding.

Peter stretched beside her, leaning back on his elbows. "I am glad to be the first."

Mary said nothing, trying hard to regain her composure and still her quaking emotions. She looked away from Peter and chose a neutral topic. "I am taking the boy with us."

"But of course."

Mary snapped around to make certain he did not jest with her. "You truly do not mind?"

Peter chuckled. "We have already amassed five. What is one more?"

Mary felt tenderness anew for the rugged knight at her side. She wished she could tell him all that she felt, but it was beyond her to know how to put any of it into words. Getting to her feet, she looked down at Peter whose passionate eyes still stirred her heart.

Not able to think of anything else, Mary confided, "I am glad you were the first, as well." Then without waiting to see his expression, she hurried back to the wagon and the children.

Peter stared after Mary with a smug smile. More confident than ever of the building emotion she felt for him, he was satisfied that she had been willing to admit pleasure in his kiss. Making his way back to the wagon, Peter was surprised when Gideon approached him with a question.

"When are you going to wed Mary?"

"What a question," Peter said, rumpling the boy's hair. "How can you be so bold?"

Gideon grinned. "We are getting a whole bunch of children," he said with a tone beyond his years. "Would it not be well to get a mother and father, as well?"

Peter shook his head. "Get on with you, Gideon. 'Twould be best we make ready to leave before Mary finds yet another child in need of a family."

They left within an hour, but after a week more on the road, the count of children in the wagon had grown to ten.

"'Tis certain the donkey will pull no more," Peter said, taking William and Sarah up on the horse with him.

"I will walk," Mary said with pleading eyes fixed firmly on Peter's face. "What is one more?" She questioned, mocking his words of a week past.

"One more will do in the beast, that is what. I pray we find that grandmother of yours soon. 'Tis getting truly difficult to feed them all."

Mary smiled. She knew Peter's gruff tone was nothing more than show. She looked back at the wagonful of children. They ranged in age from baby Anne to the ten-year-old Gwenny, who had taken it upon herself to mother all the others. If only they could find her grandmother and a home to shelter them all in. If only. . .

ten

It met with the satisfaction of both Peter and Mary when a monastery came into sight. It wasn't just any monastery, however, it was the very one in which Peter was to deliver the king's missive. They were growing ever closer to York, and with its nearness, Peter's confusion grew.

Sitting alone that night in the quiet of the abbott's study, Peter reflected on his journey north and wrote in the journal he'd kept for King Edward. The number of dead had lessened as they moved north, and to Peter's relief, they had found no more children in need of a home.

With a yawn, he rubbed his tired eyes and contemplated what he should next do. He had done as the king bade him, and now he should return to report his findings. But returning to Edward meant leaving Mary. And the children.

"Is it well with you, my son?" the abbott questioned, entering the room.

Peter suppressed another yawn. "I am nearly spent, but otherwise well. I am more relieved yet to find no sickness among your walls."

"Aye, we are most grateful to God for such a blessing."

Peter sat back and looked quizzically at the priest. "Is this illness the hand of God? His punishment upon a faithless people?"

"There are those who say it is. The Egyptians were sent plagues in the time of Moses. Still, these are not the things upon which I personally choose to concentrate. Sickness often does bring a man closer to God, and of't it brings him thoughts of his own limitations and his own death."

Peter nodded. "I confess, 'tis so with me. I lived a life of ease, and even though I lost my family at an early age, I was blessed with comfort and purpose. I have seen much and lived much, but never gave thought for the morrow because it simply did not matter."

The abbott took a seat on the bench beside Peter. "'Tis not unusual for man to think thusly. The church is always here to guide and offer direction to mankind, but without a repentant heart, there is no salvation."

"This salvation you speak of," Peter said, suddenly realizing he needed to know more, "is it that which saves man from death?"

"Not physical death," the abbott replied. "By God's Holy Scripture, man is instructed that he must die in his flesh, yet a spiritual death will follow for those without the forgiveness of Christ. For what is a man but that which makes up his spirit? The flesh is weak. 'Tis here one day and gone the next. By your own witness you have seen such a thing be true. The soul of man is that which physical death need not touch. The soul of man is that which can be given over to God in obedience to the Scripture and thus a spiritual death may be avoided."

"I have heard this within the walls of great cathedrals," Peter admitted, "yet it seemed unimportant at the time. I went to the battlefield at a young age, and there as an orphan was made squire to Robert d'Artois, a French nobleman who had won great favor with King Edward by pledging his undying support. He taught me much about warfare and fighting. I was with him when he took the city of Vannes. Scarcely a drop of English blood was spilled and even the Countess de Montfort came to offer her congratulations to d'Artois. I remember watching the pomp and ceremony and thinking, 'This is what makes a man great. This is what makes a man's life worth living.'" Peter paused, "A few weeks later, d'Artois was dead by the same men he had once defeated."

"And what thought you then?" questioned the abbott.

Peter smiled ruefully. "I thought that a man's true obligation should be to his own pleasure, for obviously life was quite undeterminable. I went back to England with d'Artois's body. Edward had requested he be buried by the Black Friars in London under great ceremony. I suppose it was then that I gave myself over to self-satisfaction and left behind all notions of the morrow."

The abbott nodded. "'Tis often the way of man. Dealing with the inevitable truth of our frailty and brief passing upon the earth causes many a man to turn to self-serving pleasure. How think you now? Now that you have witnessed even more death and destruction? Are you more convinced that life is so fleeting that you must give your every moment to selfish ambition?"

Peter shook his head. "I pray there be more."

The abbott smiled. "There is. Let me tell you about the forgiveness of God and life eternal."

※

Mary stood in a protective pose, almost as if threatened by the presence of the dark-robed men. They had just suggested that the children were the responsibility of the church and that her duty was to turn them over to the care of the monks.

"We have many in the village who would welcome the wee ones," one man argued. "They would be well cared for. What can you offer them upon the road?"

"I will not leave the children behind," Mary stated firmly. "They are as much family to me as any I have been bound to by blood."

"But mistress you have no husband," the man tried to continue without luck.

"I will not hear of it. Should you threaten me, I will

simply take them in the night and make my way to my grandmother's estate." Mary hoped the word estate would make it clear that the monks were dealing with more than a pauper.

Peter came into the argument at this point and Mary hurried to his side, pulling him with her to where the men stood. "They want to take my children," she announced possessively. "They feel it is the place of the church to provide care for the orphans. I will not hear of it. Peter," she said, turning her dark, angry eyes upward, "you will not let them take our children, will you?"

Peter put a supportive arm around Mary's thin shoulders. "Nay, we will not be parted from the children. If you will excuse us," he said to the monks and pulled Mary outside into a courtyard.

"The very nerve of those men. They believe because they are men of the church, they can force their will upon others. I will not hear of it!" She was angry and knew her temper was nothing new to Peter. "They cannot do this thing, Peter!"

"Calm down, Mary. No one is taking the children just yet."

"What do you mean, just yet?"

"I am simply saying that the matter is nowhere near the point of causing panic. You must calm yourself." He dropped his hold on her arm and motioned to a bench. "Sit here and talk to me."

Mary crossed her arms. "I do not feel like talking. I feel like leaving this place."

"Be reasonable, Mary. The children are asleep and it is quite late. I thought you would be sleeping as well."

"I might have been, but for those testy souls within. Imagine those men thinking they could do a better job in caring for the children!"

"But Mary, we have nothing to offer them. Perhaps that

is all the monks were thinking. We are not a family in the eyes of the church."

"The church! Who cares what the church thinks."

"'Tis heresy you are speaking now. Would you have them burn you at the stake for your lack of faith?"

"What of your own lack of faith?" Mary questioned, casting a sharp look down to where Peter sat.

"Mayhap my faith is not lacking now."

"Oh, so I suppose they have convinced you to see reason in their part," Mary said angrily. She felt tears come to her eyes. Would she have to face this thing alone?

"Do not be afraid," Peter said softly. "I still champion you, sweet Mary."

"I am not afraid!" Mary declared. "I will care for the children, and no one will take them from me. No one!"

Peter seemed weary as he ran a hand through his hair. "Mary, there are ten children. Mayhap giving over some to the monks is not a bad idea. They have families who work the lands here and who would care for the little ones."

Mary shook her head. "I cannot. I love them as though they were my own."

Peter nodded. "As do I. But love should not be a thing which brings harm. Would you love them at the price of their empty bellies?"

"I will care for them," Mary said with a sobbing voice.

Peter got to his feet and reached out for Mary, but she pushed him away. "Touch me not! You could give away my children without so much as a second thought. I will not have any part of you."

"They are as much my children as yours, Mary."

Trembling built up to rage. "Which would you give over, Peter? William and Sarah? Gwenny? Surely even you would have a hard time bidding Gideon farewell." In the brilliant glow of the moonlight, she saw Peter's face fall. In her heart,

Mary knew that she would regret her words, but anger pushed her forward. "Mayhap my faith is lacking, Sir Peter, but my love is not easily given, nor is it easily taken back. I will not desert these children to live in hopes of yet another who might one day love them. They are mine, surely as I am theirs. No one, not you or the monks or God Himself, will separate me from them."

eleven

Mary ignored Peter and the monks, as well, when all offered to help her in the feeding of the children the next morning. With Anne nestled in her left arm, Mary helped Gwenny to sit comfortably with the marked baby boy they now called Edward.

"I do not wish to solicit your assistance," Mary said coldly to Peter. Turning her back she muttered under her breath, "You might seek to give one of them away when my back is turned."

If Peter heard the comment, he said nothing. Mary didn't care. Her motherly instincts took over and she was determined to fight for each and every child as though they truly were her own.

When she had seated herself beside a young girl named Ellen, one of the last to join the band, Mary nodded to the children that they could eat. "Gideon, you help William and Sarah." Gideon nodded but seemed more quiet than usual. Mary feared that he was being affected by her fight with Peter, but there was no honorable way to make peace at this point and so she did nothing to ease the boy's noted concern.

Staring down the table at her little family, Mary felt strongly about her decision to keep them together. After baby Edward, they had added two sisters—Ellen and Matilda, ages nine and eight, respectively. The last two to join the group were boys. Darias, a ten year old, had been left for dead after taking on the plague. Miraculously, however, he had lived, and Peter had found him eating grass for sustenance. Smiling at the boy, Mary watched him eat porridge with a hearty appetite. Six-year-old Robert completed the group and won Mary's heart with his huge blue eyes and happy laughter. How children could laugh in the midst of such tragedy was beyond Mary's ability to reason.

The monks departed the room, but Peter remained behind. Determined to reason with Mary, Peter joined the feasting children, receiving Mary's frown as he did.

"You all look well-rested," Peter said, rumpling Darias' hair. "And I see that porridge agrees with you, Master Darias." The boy smiled up and nodded.

"Mary, it appears these children could use a bath," Peter said, and moans followed his comment around the table.

"I will see to their needs," Mary snapped.

"I only meant to offer my help. The boys might want to join me at the lake. 'Tis just beyond the dovecotes."

Mary said nothing, and Peter took her silence to be acceptance. He dished himself a bowl of porridge and took up a piece of hard bread before continuing. "We can go after we finish eating. The water will be chilly, but it will do all of us good to bathe. The good brothers of the abbey have even given me a small piece of soap."

"I said I would see to them!"

Peter met Mary's angry stare with his own mounting temper. "I care not for your protests. I am saying this. The boys will come with me to the lake after we break the fast. I will return the soap to you and you may take the girls. I will even carry Gwenny to the water for you."

Mary threw her spoon down. "I am surrounded by willful men."

"Willful men? Take a look at yourself, sweet Mary."

"Do not call me that!" she protested.

"I should not, for 'tis certainly not true this day." Peter noted Gideon's frown and the woeful stares of the others.

"I will not argue with you in front of the children."

"Good, then you will not speak with me at all, because my place is with them and I will not be taken from them. Not for bathing exercises or any other cause. Do I make myself clear?"

Peter took in the scene with reserved control. He saw no need to frighten the children. "You make yourself very clear. You are selfish and lack all common sense to make good judgement. Nevertheless, now is not the time to discuss the matter further. I am going hunting, as I promised the friars fresh game under the protective permission of King Edward. We will speak of this later."

He got up and with one last look at Mary to emphasize the seriousness of his words, he turned to leave. At the door he paused and with a slight smile he added. "'Tis most glad I am to learn of your flaws before seeking your hand in marriage. I would have been most annoyed to believe you of one character, only to find you a wife of bitter nature." With that he left the room, fully satisfied at the shocked expression on Mary's face.

Mary finished the last of the children's baths before seeing to one for herself. She was filthy and felt as though her skin crawled. It would feel wonderful to be clean again. After instructing Gideon, Darias, and Gwenny to see to the others, Mary took a linen towel and monk's robe and went to the lake. She tried not to think about the kindness of the men she'd so thoroughly offended the night before and again at breakfast. They had seen her limited wardrobe and offered her the robe to wear while her own clothes dried. The gentle-spoken abbot told her that such times made strange demands upon people. He promised to send one of the brothers into the village to seek out clothes for Mary. She had protested such a need but in her heart was thankful for the suggestion. Her own clothes were ragged and torn, and she seriously doubted they would hold up to a good washing.

It was only here, in the privacy of her bath, that Mary allowed herself to think on Peter's words. Had he been serious about seeking her hand in marriage? And what if he was? She scarcely knew the man, and while it was not uncommon for such marriages to take place, Mary had always seen herself as independent of the need to wed.

Still, in her heart, Mary knew she was lost. She cared deeply for this bedraggled knight of the realm. He had a good mind and gentle spirit, and his love for the children was evident. He'd never once lifted a hand to strike any of them, and even when Mary argued with him, he had held his temper in check.

But his words about her character, more than the idea of marriage, bothered her most. Was she a woman of bitter nature? Had the past and the scars transferred to her by an angry, embittered father, left her without a hope of gentleness?

She thought of her recent actions and in the stillness of her meditation realized how childishly she had behaved. Children must have food and shelter, as well as love and protection. *Can I give them what they need?* she wondered. *Or will my pride cost them their lives?*

She finished her tasks, and after leaving the surcoat and tunic to dry upon a bush, Mary returned to the abbey. She felt suddenly shy about facing the men, knowing full well that she'd acted poorly in their presence. But her embarrassment and concern had no time to linger.

"He stepped upon a trap," one of the monks told Mary as she came into the kitchen.

She inquired of the bleeding man now lain out upon the kitchen table. "When did he do this? Is there a doctor among you? The wound should be seared to stop the bleeding."

"We cannot do such a thing," the man responded.

Mary pushed her way through the gathering of brothers

and took the man's bleeding foot in hand. "Why are you unable to help him?" she asked of the abbott who had just arrived.

"'Tis a decree by the Council of Bayeux. In 1300 it was decided that none of the clergy could be given over to any act of surgery, including cautery and incision."

"Bah! What nonsense. The man will die if we do not help him." Mary glanced around the room and spied the linen towel she'd brought from her bath. She had still been drying her hair when the injured man's cries took her attention.

"Bring that cloth," she ordered one of the monks. Ripping a piece from the towel, Mary first tied back her still damp hair. "Now bring me a pan of water from the hearth, and you," she pointed to a young friar, "go fetch my bag." The man nodded and hurried to do as he was told.

Mary searched out the drawers of the nearest cupboard and found a large knife. Giving it over to yet another man, she directed him to put it in the fireplace coals.

Tearing more pieces of cloth, Mary dipped them in the hot water and began to clean the bleeding wound. The man cried out in his misery. "Hold him still," Mary directed, "and give him something to bite down on. This will not be a gentle task."

The abbott nodded to his men, and Mary took a cup and poured water over the gaping wound. The man screamed and fainted dead away, much to Mary's relief. She took up her bag, searched through it for a variety of bottles, and motioned a young monk to assist her. "We will make a paste of these," she said authoritatively. "Mix in a pinch of each and only enough water to make a thick paste. I will sear the flesh and apply this afterward." The man nodded and went to work.

"Bring me the knife," Mary instructed, satisfied that she had cleansed the wound as best she could. The abbott himself brought the knife and after murmuring a blessing, handed the heated blade to Mary.

"God's grace upon you, daughter."

Mary nodded, but said nothing more as she placed the blade against the torn, bleeding skin. Several monks quickly left the room at the heinous smell of burning flesh, but Mary noted that the young man worked on at making her paste, seemingly oblivious to the stench.

"Now the paste," she called and the bowl was brought to her. "You did a good job," she told the man in her way of thanks. Smearing the concoction upon the wound, Mary then bound it securely with linen and tied it snug. "'Tis not to be touched for three days." She eyed each man who remained and received solemn nods.

"You have the touch of healing from God Himself," the abbot said approvingly. "'Tis unseemly for a woman, but we are most grateful for your skills."

Mary stuffed bottles back into her bag and turned with a smirking expression. "God had naught to do with my healing skills. I learned them at my father's side." The abbot opened his mouth as if to reply, but Mary grabbed her things and stalked out of the room, unconcerned with what he might say.

Throughout the day, Mary contemplated what she might say to set things right with Peter. When nightfall came and he had not returned, Mary began to fear he had deserted them. She nervously paced the kitchen, turning from time to time to the open door. Quick glances across the field left Mary disheartened at their refusal to yield forth Peter.

"Have you supped?" the voice of the abbot sounded from behind her.

Mary turned, and having a contrite heart for her previous actions, she shook her head and moved toward the man. "I must apologize for my words earlier this day. I have not been myself, and I gave no concern for the feelings of others."

"You are forgiven, daughter. Come sup with me and tell me of your father. He must truly be a fine physician."

"He was," Mary said, nearly wincing with the memory. "He died at the hands of our villagers. They believed him to consort with the devil."

If her words shocked the abbott, he did not respond by so much as raising a bushy white eyebrow. His soft blue eyes bore into her soul, and immediately Mary felt at ease. He brought roasted meat, fresh bread, and drink to the table and waved Mary away when she sought to serve him. He blessed the food, and Mary found that his prayerful words reached deep into her heart.

"How is it that you can be certain He listens?" she questioned the abbott.

"You mean God, of course?"

Mary nodded. "I have not been brought up to have faith in that which I cannot prove or see. Heresy, perhaps, but my teacher is now dead."

"As a physician, your father could often not see the workings of man's flesh. Still, he knew that something caused the heart to beat. Did it cease to exist simply because you could not see it?"

Mary felt the first spark of understanding. "There were evidences of the heart at work. Things are different within a body in which the heart beats and one in which it has stopped."

"So to it is with the spirit. Thus the spirit into which God has breathed life is different from the one which knows Him not." The abbott paused and offered her a tender look. "You have endured much and you desire to be at peace." He sliced bread and meat and offered them to her.

"What must I do?" Mary asked, bringing her hands to her head. "I know my way is not right. I have felt it since I first spoke with the mother of baby Anne. She was a good woman who had a strong faith in eternal life. It caused me to think, but many years of my father's anger and disapproval of the church kept me from serious consideration. Then, too, is my desire to work at healing. The church frowns on the science of medicine."

"The church frowns on man putting himself above God. If God chooses to take a soul from this earth, where is it man's place to interfere?"

"But did not Christ, Himself, heal people of afflictions?"

"True enough, and the church has no argument with the physician who seeks to use prayer and the things God has given us in this earth in which to aid healing."

"But does the church believe scientific medicine such as surgery to be the work of the devil? Is it not possible for God to have given man the knowledge of this thing?"

The abbott grew thoughtful for a moment. "Good knowledge comes from God; that much is true—just as evil and chaos are weapons the devil uses. But knowledge in the hands of the wrong person can be used for evil."

"'Tis God not knowing enough to work His good in spite of these folk? Cannot a man or a woman of good heart, seeking to be in accordance with God, perform simple procedures to aid and assist the hurting and dying?"

"But when a man is appointed to die, he dies," the abbott said firmly.

"Exactly so. My surgery will not interfere with God's predestination of life or death. Is that not true?"

The abbot smiled. "You are a cunning young woman."

Mary sighed. "'Tis not my desire to be so idly, and yet in my heart I feel the need for a spiritual healing, yet always before when that emptiness made itself known I put it from me."

"And now?"

"Now, I find that I can scarce face the new day without wondering about God and what plan He might have. Will

He hear me, Father? After all these years of denial?"

"Do you desire to repent of your sins?"

Mary thought on this for a moment. "I desire to make right whatever is wrong between myself and God. I desire to know that when I pray, He hears me and not only this, but that He cares, as well."

The abbott smiled and closed a big hand over Mary's smaller one. "He hears and He cares, Mary. Repent your sins and ask for His saving grace. Christ Jesus will be your Lord and Saviour, and a home in heaven will be yours forever."

"And in honoring God with my trust, will He punish me for my desire to heal? Will I need to put such concerns aside?"

The abbott shook his head. "I believe your desire to be for good, Mary. God honors all who seek His face and strive to do His will first. If that is where your heart is, God will deal justly with your ambitions."

"Then I will trust Him."

Mary prayed, and immediately a peace such as she had never known descended upon her. She looked up at the abbott with wet eyes, feeling that deep within, she had rid herself of the creature that had once existed.

"God's love is a healing love, Mary. He makes right that which is wrong."

"But there is so much in my life to set right," Mary said honestly. With a sad glance over her shoulder at the empty open door, Mary felt her tears fall anew. "I fear I have wounded with my words."

"Wounds need but a bit of care, no?"

"I drove Peter away with my harshness," she admitted. "Mayhap he will not forgive me for such a fit of temper."

"Were your words unjust?"

"Aye," Mary replied. "I felt he did not understand my love for the children, yet I know it not to be true. He loves them as well, and it would tear at his heart to see a single one of them misplaced."

The abbott nodded, seeming to understand her plight. "You spoke out of fear and not out of trust."

"'Tis hard to trust," Mary confessed. "But my love bids me to do so."

"Your love for the children?"

"Nay," she answered, wiping at her tears. "My love for Peter."

The old man's face broke into a wide grin. "You have given your heart to that young man?"

"I fear 'tis true enough for all the good it might now do," Mary replied. "We know so little of each other, yet a strong bond grew. I pray I have not destroyed it, for I love Peter with all my heart."

"'Tis a good thing," Peter's voice called out from the doorway, "for it might help me in winning the king's permission to make you my wife."

Mary jumped to her feet and turned to face him. He was filthy from his hunt and exhaustion could clearly be read in his eyes, but there was joy in them as well.

"Oh, Peter!" she exclaimed, both embarrassed and happy that he'd overheard her confession. "You were gone so long. I had begun to despair of your return. Are you well? Did you have trouble?" She paused with a sudden understanding of his declaration. "Make me your wife?"

Peter laughed out loud, and even the abbott chuckled from behind her. Mary shook her head, fearful that she'd dreamed the entire thing. "Did you truly say—"

"Aye," Peter interrupted, stepping forward to take hold of Mary. She was glad for the clean clothes brought to her by the monks and hoped Peter found them fetching on her as he scrutinized her from head to toe. "The bath seems to suit you well. I do not remember these clothes, but they pale in comparison to your beauty."

"Oh, Peter," she said with a sigh. "I am sorry for my harsh tongue. I drove you away, and it frightened me through and through."

He touched her cheek lightly. "'Tis forgotten and forgiven."

"But I should make it up to you."

Peter grinned. "You may start by saying yea to my proposal."

Mary felt her pulse quicken. "You were serious then?"

"As serious as a man can possibly be about the woman he loves."

"Loves?" Mary swallowed hard. "You love me?"

"I would not wed you unless I did," he replied somewhat harshly, then softened, pulling her near. "Aye, I love you, sweet Mary, and I want nothing more than to know you better and help you care for that growing brood."

"I love you, Peter," she said with such joy that she thought she might burst into tears anew.

"Is that a yes?"

She nodded, dark hair dancing behind her.

twelve

Gideon peered eagerly into the faces of his conspirators early the next morning. "You have to do this," he said, trying hard to sound older than his eight years. "Mary and Peter will never get married and keep us if we do not help them get back together."

"But what have we do with this?" Gwenny asked, doubting Gideon's reason.

Gideon's glance darted from Darias to Gwenny and then to Matilda and Ellen. As the oldest of the ten, Gideon had chosen them to listen to his plan.

"Mary and Peter have been fighting," he began, and all heads nodded in acknowledgment. "They really love each other, and I think they will be our father and mother, but only if they stop fighting."

"They are adults, and we are but children," Darias chimed in. "We cannot make them marry."

Gideon sighed. "Mayhap we are children, but do not children need parents?"

"Aye," Gwenny replied. "We need them, but we have lost parents before. Why should we think to have parents again?"

"Because I prayed," Gideon answered confidently and looked to each eager face as if to reaffirm his words.

"I have been with Peter since the beginning, when there were no other children," Gideon continued. "That makes me the leader."

"What are your plans?" Darias asked in a way that showed acceptance of Gideon's predetermined position.

"I am going into the woods. I will hide there, and you will

111

tell Peter and Mary that I have gone. Tell them that I was sad because they were fighting. Tell them that I want them to be my mother and father. Tell them 'tis what we all want."

Ellen and Matilda remained silent, but Gwenny was still unconvinced. "You could be eaten alive by some animal," she suggested.

"Nay, 'tis morning and they will be full from eating all night long."

"Would it not be safer to stay here and just tell them we want them to wed and care for us always?" she questioned.

"Nay!" Gideon's exasperation with the group was starting to show. His eight-year-old face took on a worried expression that seemed as grave as his words. "They will not listen right now. They are mad, and when you are mad, you do not listen."

"'Tis true enough," Darias stated as one who knew. "I cannot listen when I am mad."

"See?" Gideon said, looking to Gwenny. "'Tis true." He looked nervously around the room to where the others played in silence. "They are too little to be left alone. We must not let the monks take them away."

Gwenny looked defensively to where Anne slept at her feet. "No one will take little Anne away. I will not let them."

"But we are only children, and big folks seldom listen to us."

"So you will run away to the woods," Gwenny began, "and when Mary notices that you are gone, we are to tell her that you were afraid?"

"No," Gideon replied patiently, "tell them together. Make Peter and Mary both come to hear what I told you."

Gwenny and Darias exchanged a glance and then nodded at Gideon. His face lit up as he realized they would do their part in his scheme.

"Now remember, do not tell them until time to eat, else I

will not have enough time to hide," Gideon reminded the group.

Gideon had been gone for over an hour when Mary appeared at the door to call the children to the morning meal. Making a routine counting of heads, Mary noted that Gideon was missing from the group. No doubt the boy had made his way to Peter's side.

"'Tis time for breakfast," Mary announced. Coming to Gwenny's side, she reached down and took Anne. "I will fetch Peter to carry you to the table, Gwenny."

The girl nodded but refused to meet Mary's eyes. Darias, only a few feet away, kept his gaze on the floor and went to retrieve Edward.

"You are most unusually quiet this morning," Mary said cautiously. She looked at each of the somber faces and worried that her fight with Peter had caused them all to fear her. "What is it that vexes you so?"

When no one answered, Mary truly began to worry. Anne cooed softly in her arms, but otherwise even Edward remained still. Looking from one child to the next, Mary felt her breath catch in her throat.

"Has something happened that I should know about?

Gwenny looked up at Darias and then to Mary. Slowly she nodded her head.

"Tell me then!" Mary commanded a bit louder than she'd intended. "Tell me now."

"We cannot," Gwenny finally spoke. "Peter must be here too."

"What say you?" Mary questioned, tightening her hold on Anne. The baby began to protest with a screech of indignation. Mary lessened her grip and drew in a deep breath. "Where is Gideon? Has this to do with him?"

"Aye," Gwenny replied. "But he bid us to silence unless you and Peter were both here."

Mary nodded curtly and went in search of Peter.

"Peter! Peter!" she cried his name aloud. Her voice frightened Anne to tears. Trying to hush the child and still call out, Mary gave up and let Anne cry. Where could Peter have gotten off to? Better yet, where had Gideon gotten off to?

'Tis foolishness to worry, Mary told herself. *Gideon is probably just playing a game with us.* But in her heart she knew it wasn't the case. Gideon had taken her fight with Peter most personally. He alone had been her mainstay in the early days when Peter had been so sick. He alone knew how much Mary and Peter had come to care for each other.

"Peter!" She was growing desperate and began to search the yards behind the guest house. Tears formed in her eyes. Gideon had to be all right. He just had to be.

Anne's incessant wailing announced their arrival to the malthouse. *Peter just has to be here,* Mary thought and pled with God to make it so.

"Peter!"

The large empty room filled immediately with echoes of the baby's lusty cry. A quick glance confirmed that no one was there.

Mary's tears began to fall in earnest as she continued her search. Her imagination ran wild with images of Gideon lying hurt and defenseless in the woods. The distant sound of the river caused her to shudder with thoughts of the boy's lifeless body washing to shore.

"Peter!" she called out against her sobs. "Peter!"

ת

Peter's skin was nearly blue when he emerged from the river. He'd taken the quiet hours of the morning to slip away from the others and bathe. His mind reflected on the events of the past few days.

He was to marry. He'd actually asked a woman to be his mate. Somehow the idea was not nearly as foreign as he'd imagined it might be. He thought of Mary and her long dark tresses. He imagined the violet eyes and dark sooty lashes. She'd bewitched him with her girlish smiles and gentle touch, and now she was to become his wife. What a wonder!

The responsibility of such a thing was never far from his thoughts. Toweling dry, Peter thought of the multitude of children who now were in his charge. He'd led men upon the battlefield, sometimes to victory and oft' times to fall back and fight another day, but never had such a task loomed at him with this depth of solemnity. Children needed a great deal of care, and while Mary was quite willing to give herself over to the task, she could not possibly provide for their nourishment and shelter. No, that responsibility would be Peter's, and how could he give himself over to it without lands of his own and a place to call home?

These new thoughts caused him no small amount of concern. Would Edward be willing to give him leave from the battlefield in order to settle an estate of his own? Surely with this blight upon England having claimed so many lives, Edward would see the need to begin again. Peter could benefit not only his newly acquired family, but others as well. Perhaps he could take up established lands and see that crops and livestock once again thrived.

These new thoughts intrigued him. Dressing quickly to ward off the morning chill, Peter had just taken a seat on the ground when he caught the faint sound of someone calling his name. Quickly he pulled on his boots, secured his belt and sword, and gathered up his belongings.

"Peter!" It was Mary. "Peter!" She called again and he thought he denoted desperation in her tone.

A feeling of dread washed over him. Perhaps someone had fallen ill. Perhaps it was one of the children. Peter quickened his steps and through his mind ran imagines of the children. Darias with his bowl-style haircut and huge brown eyes. Gwenny, hobbling with the crutches Peter had devised.

"Peter!" The voice tore at his heart.

"I'm here, Mary!" he called, and in his mind he saw each of the children. Ellen and Matilda, such tiny mites with dark blue eyes and pale complexions. Robert, independent for his six years and willfully stubborn. William, Sarah, and the babies Edward and Anne. "Dear God," he panted the prayer, "do not let harm have come to the children."

He ran through the brush, mindless of the branches that beat at him in his passage. He burst into the clearing and saw Mary with Anne bundled against her, rushing across the empty field to him. It was then that Gideon's face came to mind, and somehow Peter knew her news had to do with the blond-haired boy.

When she reached him, Mary collapsed into Peter's arms. Anne objected with her howls and cries, but both adults ignored the baby and clung to each other.

"Gideon?" Peter questioned, and Mary nodded breathlessly.

"The children," she gasped out, trying to regain her breath.

"What of the children? What of Gideon?" Peter had taken a firm grip of her shoulders. His face softened tenderly as he saw the misery in her eyes. "'Twill be alright, sweet Mary," he whispered.

"He is not with the others," Mary finally managed to say. Anne settled a bit as Mary's voice calmed. "Gwenny told me he wanted us to hear the news together. I believe he has run away."

Peter took Anne in one arm and pulled Mary along with him. "We had best find out what the boy is up to," he said.

"Oh, Peter. I think he is worried about our fight. I saw how he looked when I argued with you, and he has no way to know that we have made up our differences."

"That may well be the case," Peter replied, "but he has no cause to grieve you like this."

Peter's eyes took in the landscape around them. The monastery held an abundant number of hiding places. Beyond the walls of the abbey were forests, field, and the river from which he'd just come. There was no real way of knowing where the small boy might have taken himself off to.

The expression on the faces of the other children told Peter all he needed to know. Gwenny sat quietly playing with Edward, while the other children, seeming to sense the gravity of the situation, sat silently watching and waiting.

"What is this that you must tell us?" Peter asked the children collectively.

Gwenny darted a look to Darias and back again to Peter and Mary. "He has gone away."

Peter felt Mary stiffen at his side. "Did he say where he was to go and why?" Peter questioned.

"He went to the woods," Darias offered. "He thinks it will make you. . . ." He fell silent and looked imploringly to Gwenny to finish.

"He feared you would give us over to the monks," Gwenny finally managed. She put Edward down to toddle across the floor in awkward baby steps. "You would not do that, would you?"

"Of course not. What made him think this?" Peter's words were soft as he knelt beside the girl.

"You and Mary were fighting, and it scared him," Gwenny said, then lowered her eyes and added, "It scared me too."

"But why Gwenny? We would not hurt you."

"Gideon said you and Mary were our only hope of staying together," Gwenny confided. Her eyes were huge and mournful. "He, that is we, want to stay with you. We have no kin and no place to go. If you do not wed and take us with you, we will have to stay here."

"I will never leave you here," Mary interjected before Peter could speak. "I could not leave you."

"Nor I," Peter agreed.

"Gideon thought if you saw how much we wanted to stay with you, how strong we felt," Darias finally spoke, "he figured you would keep together and not fight."

Peter chuckled in spite of the somber moment. "I would imagine even together, Mary and I will have our moments of disagreement." Getting up, Peter bent over and lifted Gwenny. "Your breakfast is getting cold. You must eat while Mary and I decide what is to be done.

Darias grabbed Edward, while the other children shuffled up to stand before Mary and Peter. Warm love for the children flooded Peter's soul. They were perfectly helpless without him, and their faces bespoke of such trust that Peter's heart swelled with pride. The urgency to find Gideon surged through him like fire.

Ushering the children to breakfast and leaving them to the ministerings of the monks, Peter motion Mary outside.

"I am going to go look for Gideon. I do not imagine him to have gotten far." Mary nodded, and worry lined her expression.

Peter reached a hand to her cheek, still amazed at the softness of her skin. Her eyes darkened with emotion at his touch. "Fear not, my love," he said, feeling Mary tremble beneath his touch. "I will find our boy."

Mary sighed. "I know you will."

Peter longed to kiss her, but instead reluctantly released her. "I had best go."

Mary watched him trot off in the direction of the nearest trees. Thick undergrowth and brush kept her eyes from being able to search beyond the first tall oaks.

"Most precious Father," she whispered as Peter disappeared into the woods, "please keep them safe and bring them back to me." The chill autumn wind picked up and stung her cheeks. With a weary glance at the overcast skies, Mary added, "And please hurry."

thirteen

Peter saw the signs of Gideon's passage and breathed a sigh of relief. Following the well-laid trail, Peter called out to the boy.

"Gideon! Gideon if you can hear me, please answer!"

Silence greet him, and the shroud-like cover of the forest's ceiling made Peter pause to listen for any sound. Every breath he drew echoed in the stillness. When the wind picked up, Peter could see the rustling of the tree tops, but little else. Here in the deep coverage of the forest it was dark and damp but well-protected from the ravages of the wind.

Silently, Peter prayed for guidance before continuing. Prayer and trust in God were things so new to him that Peter often forgot their importance. It seemed odd, he thought, that so many years of knightly service should surround him with religious rhetoric and yet leave not a single mark upon his soul. It took, instead, the devastation of nations by a disease no one understood to even give him cause to think upon God and what might lie beyond this earth.

Pressing forward, Peter followed the beaten-down pathway where twigs had been snapped in two and the undergrowth had been clearly tread upon. The trail was leading him back to the river, and Peter felt a shudder of apprehension run up his spine at the thought of Gideon helplessly trying to master the river's swift current.

"Gideon!" he called out, hurrying his step.

The sound of the river grew louder. The water could have been a soothing sound as it fell against the stones and hurried its way downstream. It could have been had the moment not been so serious.

Peter glanced quickly up stream. The trees thinned out but still lined the banks. Overhead, a heavy gray sky promised rain, and Peter knew he had to hurry.

Downstream seemed more heavily overgrown and looked the most likely place for a small boy to hide. Choosing that direction, Peter was soon rewarded with a small set of footprints in the mud.

"Gideon!"

The water rushed by, blocking out all other sound, and Peter strained his ear for any murmur or noise which might betray the boy's presence. The wind was able to reach him and so too, the first drops of rain.

There was nothing to do but go forward. Peter could hardly leave the boy to fend for himself. As the rain increased, Peter longed for the comfort of a warm fire and Mary at his side.

With rain making it difficult to see, Peter pulled close the hood of his cloak and fought to make out the trail. Small prints led down to the water's edge where it appeared to Peter that Gideon had attempted to cross the water. There was no way of knowing what had happened, whether the current had been too swift or the water too cold, but prints led away from the water and down the bank.

Silently thanking God, Peter wiped water from his face and moved ahead. When the muddy prints headed back to the safety of the forest, Peter was again thankful.

"Gideon!" Peter called out when he'd come a short way into the woods.

"Peter? Is that you?" the small, uncertain voice called back.

"Gideon, where are you? Come out this instant!"

Peter glanced quickly around the shadowy haven. In a moment, Gideon emerged from the undergrowth with a sheepish look on his face. Peter could tell from the look of the boy that he feared he might well be in deep trouble.

"Where's Mary?" Gideon asked, looking behind Peter as

if he expected to see her standing there.

"She is back at the monastery, where you should be," Peter admonished. "You could not possibly desire she risk her life as you have your own, in order to be here."

Gideon's expression sobered considerably. "I did not want you to go away, Peter."

Peter felt his fear and anxiety melt away. He could not be angry at Gideon, and he opened his arms to the child. Gideon rushed to the knight and clung tightly to his neck when Peter lifted him into the air.

"You promised you would stay with me," Gideon said, pulling away just enough to see Peter's eyes.

"Aye, I promised. And I kept my word. I did not leave, but you, my good sir, did."

"I felt bad you and Mary were fighting. I was afraid you would leave us with the monks and go away," Gideon said with tears in his eyes.

Peter could hardly bear the fear he saw in the child's eyes. "I am a man of my word, Gideon. I told you I would not leave you, and I will not. At least not until I can make a home for you and the others."

"Mary, too?" Gideon asked with a voice that betrayed his fear of the answer.

"Aye, Mary too. I have asked her to be my wife and she has consented."

"Does that mean she said yes?" Gideon's eyes were hopeful.

Peter laughed aloud. "That it does, my boy. That it does."

"And you will keep all of us with you?"

"Aye, Gideon. I will make a home for all of you and any more that come our way."

The boy squealed his delight and wrapped his arms even tighter around Peter's neck.

"I see this meets with your approval," Peter said, making his way through the trees. "Let us return to the others and show Mary you are safe. You have sorely grieved her heart, and you owe her an apology."

Gideon's joy left him, and he again pulled back from Peter. "I did not mean to make her sad."

"A good man does not set out to mindlessly hurt others. Our womenfolk must be protected and cared for. They are very precious, Gideon, and we have an important job to keep them safe and provide for their needs." Gideon nodded as if he knew exactly what was expected of him. Peter continued. "Women are wondrous creatures, Gideon. They are one of God's very best gifts to the world. They love with the very depths of their hearts and when that love is taken away, they bear the scars of that wound."

"Is Mary's heart hurt?" Gideon asked with grave concern.

"Aye," Peter replied. "Her heart was near to breaking for your absence. She felt responsible because she had argued with me in front of you."

Gideon lowered his eyes. "I thought I did a good thing, Peter. I did not mean to hurt Mary's heart."

"When you see her, Gideon, you be sure and let her know how you feel."

"Will her heart get better?" he asked hopefully. "If I tell her I am sorry, will that help her not hurt?"

"Aye, Gideon," Peter answered softly. "Aye, it will help a great deal."

&

The rain saturated the ground in torrents, and Mary feared for Peter and Gideon's health. She paced the room, watching and waiting for their return, always a prayer upon her lips for their safety.

The children played quietly, sensing Mary's fear. Even Anne and Edward were silent, having fallen asleep some time back to the steady rhythm of Mary's feet pacing upon the stone floor.

Then, just as she had begun to despair, Peter came through

the door with Gideon wrapped tightly beneath his cloak.

"Oh, Gideon! Peter!" she exclaimed and went to take the boy from Peter's arms. She looked him over for any signs of harm, and when she was satisfied that there were none, she hugged him long and hard.

"I was so afraid," she murmured against Gideon's face. "I prayed and prayed, and now here you are safe and sound." She glanced up to see Peter's tender expression. "Oh, thank you, Peter for finding him. I do not wish to think what life would have been without Gideon." Tears of relief and joy streamed down her face.

Gideon reached out his hand to Mary's face. "Peter said that I hurt your heart when I ran away."

"Aye, Gideon. That you did," Mary replied with a quick knowing glance at Peter.

"I am sorry, Mary," Gideon said, tears were welling up in his eyes. "I only wanted you and Peter to stay together. I only wanted all of us to stay together.

By this time the other children had wandered over to where Mary and Gideon clung to each other. Gwenny was the first to speak.

"Aye, we want to be a family."

"With Peter for our father and you for our mother," Gideon added quickly.

"We do not want to stay with the monks," Darias interjected. "We do not want to leave you."

"You will not leave me," Mary stated firmly. Her voice took on an air of authority. "I will fight to keep you with me. Every single one of you. I love you all so very much. I cannot imagine my life without you in it. If even one of you was gone, it would make an empty place in my heart."

"Then you will be our mother?" Gwenny asked hopefully.

"I will be your mother," Mary confirmed.

"And I will be your father," Peter said, coming to put a hand on Mary's shoulder.

At this, Mary released Gideon and stood to meet Peter's gaze. "We will marry and make a home for all of you."

The children rushed around them with small arms extended to embrace the already embracing couple.

"We are going to be a family." Gideon said happily, putting first one hand in Peter's hand and the other in Mary's.

That night, after all the children were asleep, Peter motioned Mary to follow him. Mary wondered to herself what possible problem they would now have to deal with, but when she closed the door behind her, Peter swept her into his arms and kissed her soundly.

"Peter Donne!" she exclaimed in mock horror. "You have no right to take such liberties."

Peter laughed and pulled her tighter. "I have longed to kiss those cherry lips of yours since you first appeared in the fields this morning."

"It seems like a lifetime ago," Mary said, feeling suddenly flushed. "But," she added shyly, "truth be told, I have hoped for such a kiss as this from you."

"We've a great deal to discuss, my Mary."

Peter's fingers trailed up her arm spreading warmth wherever they lingered. Mary found it nearly impossible to think.

"I suppose 'tis true enough. We have fingers, I mean further to go," she said, coughing nervously at her mistake.

"Ah, Mary," Peter moaned her name and released her. "Let us seek out the abbott tonight and wed."

Mary began to tremble anew at this thought, but realized the impossibility of the matter. "You belong to Edward. 'Tis his permission you need to seek."

"I belong to you," he said, leaning forward with a suggestive grin. "And I would have you belong to me for now and all time."

Mary giggled nervously to break the tension of the moment. "You may live to regret such a desire."

"Never!" Peter exclaimed and again pulled her close.

Mary relished the scent of him and the warmth of his sinewy arms as they engulfed her body. "Will the King allow you to wed?" she asked, hesitating to mention anything which might give Peter cause to recant his declaration of love.

"Edward will see the sense in it. I am going to seek him out just as soon as we reach your grandmother's estate. 'Tis not far from here."

Mary jumped back in surprise. "You know of my grandmother?"

Peter smiled. "I questioned the abbot. He knew well of Lady Elizabeth Beckett. She is alive and well on estates just north of this place. 'Tis no more than two days walk."

"Two days? You knew this and told me naught?"

"Forgive me, but I had much on my mind."

Mary seemed stupefied at the news. "My grandmother is alive."

"She is as far as the abbot knows."

"Can we leave on the morrow?" Mary felt her breath catch in her throat. Her stomach churned nervously.

"Can you be ready on the morrow?" Peter asked teasingly.

"I can be ready now," Mary stated firmly. Then with a glance backward to the closed door, she sighed. "But 'twould be unfair to wake up the children because of my impatience. I can wait until daylight."

Peter's eyes grew dark with passion. He leaned down and placed a long, lingering kiss upon Mary's lips before speaking. "And I can wait for Edward's blessing, although I will not promise to be a patient man about the delay."

Later that evening, Mary lay down to sleep and found her mind on the trip to come. *What manner of woman will she be?* Mary wondered of her grandmother. She'd only heard her father's negative comments regarding Lady Beckett's religious faith. She couldn't remember a single kind word or fond memory of the woman. Always, her father had issued conversation regarding his mother with a bitterness and regret that threatened to swallow him up.

"Oh, Father in heaven," Mary whispered in the inky blackness of her room, "please make a way for my grandmother and me to come together. I am so afraid." She pulled the cover to her chin and trembled.

Grandmother is all I have left, she thought silently, and then a warm memory of Peter's lips upon hers came to mind. Behind this came the vision of ten little faces and their happy, trusting expressions when Mary had pledged herself to be their mother.

"I have made myself accountable for much, have I not?" she breathed the question and gave a heavy sigh. A ripple of fear shot through her as she contemplated the awesome responsibility of caring for the children.

"Dear God," she whispered, "please guide me and let me deal wisely with the children and their needs."

Finally giving in to the exhaustion of the day, Mary slept with visions of the road to come.

The next morning, Mary was overwhelmed by the kindness of the monks and abbot. The men had chosen to provide a more sturdy wagon and an elderly, but agile, mare to pull it. There was plenty of room for everyone, and Mary found herself hugging the abbot without thought.

"Thank you so very much," she said with complete sincerity. "You have given me more than I could have ever imagined."

The abbot smiled. "God's ways are not always imagined or understood. But if we trust and allow Him to work His great wonders, we see that we are well cared for and every needed thing is no farther away than a prayer."

Mary nodded. "Thank you." With Peter's help, she climbed into the wagon and took up the reins.

"Are you ready, milady?" Peter questioned with a wink.

"I am, good sire."

Peter gave a brief bow and stepped up onto his mount. "Then let us press forth into the future and what awaits us there."

fourteen

The Yorkshire countryside had not seen the devastation of the plague in the same way southern England had. There had been cases of the disease, but for the most part it was more isolated and far less consuming.

Mary watched the open country with great interest. She'd never seen the moors, but had heard her father talk much about roaming the hillsides during his youth. Rocky ravines occasionally broke the monotony of the endless gray hills, but trees were few. She tried to imagine it green and flowering, but the bitter wind made those thoughts quickly fade.

With the damp chill of winter upon them and the rains coming more and more often, Mary became gravely concerned for the children. The monks had provided blankets of wool for the trip and they helped greatly to keep the children warm, but Mary knew they needed a home and shelter. *Will Grandmother take us in?* she wondered with a side glance to where Anne slept. The baby was nearing three months of age, and Mary found it hard to accept the changes that had taken place in such a short time.

She looked to the man ahead of her. Peter rode in regal style upon his steed, and Mary's heart quickened at the sight of him. Only a few short months before, she'd not known of Peter Donne, and now, now she was pledging herself to become his wife. Had she made the right choice? Had she agreed only for the protection of the children? The questions haunted her in earnest.

They stopped for the night in a small borough where the only inn had two rooms and both were taken. Peter tried unsuccessfully to barter for the rooms and finally accepted the stable as lodging.

"The innkeeper says there is a fine loft above the livery," Peter told Mary. "The roof is sound and the sweet hay there will make ample beds and keep us warm."

Mary looked at the exhausted children and nodded. "I suppose we have no other choice. We cannot very well press on, only to end up without shelter of any kind."

"I will carry the little ones up. You go ahead with the blankets and make it ready for them."

Mary looked at Peter and noted the weariness in his eyes. "You look as though I should make a place ready for you," Mary teased.

Peter scratched his bearded face and gave a lop-sided grin. "I would rather a hot bath and a shave. I grow weary of this beard."

Just then Anne began to cry. Mary knew it was well past her feeding time. As if inspired, Edward too began to fuss. "I will care for the babies first. Bring Gwenny up, and she can help me."

When all the children were cared for and sleeping soundly in the hay, Mary asked Peter to watch over them and disappeared from the loft for a short time. When she returned, she brought a pan of hot water and a towel.

"'Tis no bath," she said with a grin, "but 'twill suffice for me to shave that face of yours."

Peter leaned up from where he'd stretched out. With a quizzical look he questioned, "You? I should let you shave me?"

Mary's smile broadened. "I shaved my father's face daily. You will prove to be no great challenge after dealing with him." Peter shook his head and dark brown hair fell across his eyes. "A haircut might also be in order," Mary added and motioned Peter to a small milking stool.

"Did you think to bring shears as well?" he quipped and

dragged himself to where Mary stood.

"Nay, but I believe there is pair in the stable below for shearing the sheep. 'Twould be simple enough to pretend you were just one more woolly creature."

Peter laughed and pulled Mary close. "You are a charming nymph, Mary Beckett. How is it that I am fortunate enough after a life of pursuit in kingly courts, to manage to convince a woman like you to be my wife?"

Mary pushed him away and pointed to the ground. "We are not wed yet, Sir Donne. Now sit and let me be about my task."

Mary placed a hot, wet towel upon Peter's face and went to retrieve the knife. She thought of Peter's words just moments earlier and couldn't help but ask, "What women pursued you in Edward's court?"

She wasn't certain, but she thought she heard him question her jealousy from beneath the towel's muffling. Stripping the towel from his face, she stared down into his dark eyes and questioned him again. "What of it, Peter?"

He smiled. "Mayhap I should wait until after you have shaved me," he said, noting the knife in her hands.

"Very well," Mary replied and went to work, "but I intend to know."

They sat side by side after Mary had finished. She was pleased with her job, having not nicked Peter's face even once. She had even managed to trim his hair using the same knife with which she'd shaved his face. He looked like a new man, and Mary was very pleased with the results.

"Now tell me of your life before the fever came," she insisted.

Peter's face took on a distinctly distant look. "I grew up around the court of Edward. I was always cared and well-provided for. I never knew want with one exception."

"And what was that?"

"Affection." Peter said thoughtfully. "Love."

Mary looked at him earnestly and realized he was quite serious. "But a man such as yourself. . ."

"Had many admirers and pursuers. That much is true," he said, not boasting in the least. "But I had never to wonder at the reason they strived to snag me. Women were plentiful." He paused for a moment as if traveling back to another lifetime. "Beauty was everywhere, and death was not a concern. At least not in the manner of today. There were always battles to fight and such, but the all-consuming fever and death were no concern to us. We were untouched by that which could harm. At least we deemed ourselves to be so."

Mary listened intently and watched Peter's face as he continued. "Velvet- and satin-clad women were everywhere. Gold and silver adorned every single person, and there was no place to set your gaze upon which did not speak of all that was good in life.

"I had my pick of silken-clothed beauties," he remarked, and Mary immediately touched the ragged wool of her own clothing. Suddenly she felt inadequate. She'd grown up with more than most in her village, but she was not affluent enough to boast of silks and satins, dripping with gold trimmings. How could Peter possibly give all of that up for the likes of a physician's daughter? Why, he might very well be given in marriage to a woman of real means and know a title and lands so vast he would always know comfort. What could she possibly offer him?

Mary was so lost in thought she hadn't realized Peter had stopped talking. He now looked at her with passion-filled brown eyes. Swallowing hard, Mary blinked back tears and forced her worried thoughts to the back of her mind. Peter, however, seemed to know where her imagination had taken her.

"There were none who could compare to you, sweet Mary," he whispered.

Mary forgot herself. "But I have naught to give you. No dowry, no lands, not even a name of well-being." She fidgeted with her skirt before continuing. "I had not thought of all you would give up by marrying me."

Peter chuckled softly. "I would give up treacherous, traitorous hearts. Women who only sought their best advantages. Women who knew naught of love, but everything of greed."

"I do not understand," Mary said in a soft, sad voice.

Peter reached out to still her hand. "Mary, you are so much more than those women. You have come to understand about life and death in a way that they never stop to consider. I have watched you give of yourself until there was naught left to give. I have seen you risk your own life and well-being to care for complete strangers. Your heart is of finer gold than the gowns of those in court. Your thoughts are of purer silver and your eyes are the richest of jewels."

"Peter, be reasonable," Mary said amid his words of poetry. "You are a knight of the King and entitled to much, much more than you will know with me. I have no real silver or gold."

"One need not possess silver and gold in order to love," Peter said, stroking her hand with his thumb. "One need only to possess a heart filled with love. Have ye a heart for me, Mary?"

The stroke of Peter's thumb upon her hand caused a tingling sensation to run up her arm. She lowered her eyes. "Aye, I have a heart for you."

Peter ran his fingers up her arm to Mary's face. Gently, he lifted her chin. Mary saw the expression of boundless love in his eyes and her heart filled with longing.

"'Tis all we need," he assured her. "My heart is yours and your heart is mine. Naught else matters."

Mary reached her hand to his clean-shaven cheek. "The little ones need clothing and shoes. They need food in their bellies and shelter overhead. You were once the reasonable one of us." She paused with a smile. "Now it would seem that task falls to me."

"Nay," Peter replied. "I am still most reasonable. I know these concerns of yours, and I will provide for them. That, my Mary, is my responsibility. I will not have you fret so. Trust me. Trust me to see to the needs that you speak of."

"Would not a court of silver and gold be of more ease and comfort?" she whispered. "I want only that you would be certain of this union. Mayhap the King will not approve of your desires. Have you considered this matter?"

Peter nodded. "I have. I know my king, and he will hear my reasons, all ten, no, eleven of them."

Mary ran her hand down the side of his face and Peter quickly captured her hand and kissed her fingers one by one.

"I love you, Peter," she whispered and let him pull her forward for a kiss.

She wrapped her arms round him, letting her hands play with the curls of hair which touched his collar. He kissed her with a tenderness that melted away Mary's concerns. *He loves me,* she thought and reveled in the knowledge. *He loves me more than silver and gold. He loves me more than the women in velvet and silk. He loves me.*

Mary slept soundly after taking her place between Anne and Edward. Peter slept near the loft ladder even though Mary had feared he'd roll off the edge in the night and plunge to severe injury on the stone floor below.

The next morning, the children sensed Mary's anticipation, and when they were once again on the rode to York, Gideon's animation got the best of him.

"Will we live with your grandmother?" he asked in eager fascination.

"It is my hope she will take us in," Mary replied, giving the old mare her head. Peter rode ahead of them as always, and Mary knew the horse would not get far, should she be of a mind to head away from the road.

"I do not know my grandmother, Gideon. My father and I never journeyed to see her. I have heard very little of her, but it is my prayer that she has a kind heart and a generous spirit."

"Will you and Peter marry in York?"

"I cannot say," Mary replied. Her wistful glance to Peter's back was not lost by Gideon's watchful eye.

"I am glad you love Peter. I love him too, and I am going to ask him if I can call him Papa instead of Peter."

"I think he would like that, Gideon. He loves you a great deal," Mary said and leaned down to whisper. "You will always be very special to him because you were the first."

Gideon's eyes brightened. "He told me I might one day be a knight. I want Peter to be proud of me. I want you to be proud of me, too."

Mary tousled his hair. "I am proud of you, Gideon. You saw things of great importance before either Peter or I could see them for ourselves. You are special to me as well, and I love you very much."

Gideon grew sober for a moment. "I never knew my father, but my mama was always with me. Do you think she would care if I called you mama, now?"

Mary looked away quickly to avoid letting Gideon see the tears that came to her eyes. "I am sure she would only want for you to be happy and loved."

"Then she would be glad I am with you and Peter, Mama." Gideon squeezed closer to Mary and put his hand in hers.

Mary could find no words to express her heart. She lightly squeezed the boy's hand and held it in her lap for a long time.

Spying a band of travelers ahead of them, Peter rode on to catch up with them and learn of their plight.

"We are bound for the Lady of the Moors," a toothless woman crooned. "We have sick and injured among us. Some have not lasted the journey."

"I have a healer with me," Peter said, motioning back to the wagon. "She is quite skilled in a variety of treatments. Perhaps those in your number who are nearing death would best be tended by her."

The old woman nodded. "We have a several who are gravely ill."

"Is it the fever?"

"Nay, leastwise not the fever from across the sea. 'Tis another matter."

Peter noted the approaching stream. "I will fetch my lady and see if she can help. Why don't you set up camp over there by the water? We will join you shortly." He reined his horse back and made his way to Mary and the children.

"There is great sickness in their group," he informed Mary. "I thought perhaps with the sun getting so low, we might make camp and you could tend them."

Mary nodded. "But why are they upon the rode?"

"They were making a pilgrimage to the Lady of the Moors."

Mary's eyes widened. "I have heard of this woman. She is said to be a great healer and," Mary added with a smile of understanding, "one who talks to God and to whom He listens."

Peter smiled. "Mayhap you two will meet and you can share your secrets."

Mary observed the people ahead as they set out to make camp. "Mayhap."

"I will set our camp away from them," Peter said without waiting for Mary's thought on the matter. "There is no sense in the children becoming ill as well."

"But I may be a long while with the others," Mary said, noting the numbers. There were at least twenty people in the group.

"I will be fine. Gwenny will help with the babies."

"I can help too," Gideon said suddenly. "I helped first with Anne, remember?"

Peter nodded. "Of course, and I will depend on you to honor your word and give me your best." Gideon beamed.

Peter arranged their camp while Mary gathered her things and left final instructions with the older children. Making her way to the ragged group, she wondered how to best serve their needs.

"I am Mary," she told the toothless woman.

"I am Margaret of Derby. We travel with our sick to the Lady of the Moors."

"I see. Are there those here who I might help?"

The woman nodded and pointed a crooked finger to where a group of people lay upon the ground. "They are not long for the world."

With a prayer in her heart, Mary went quickly to her task. They were to remain at the camp for three more days. The people who Mary nursed were gravely ill and further travel was deemed impossible. Some of the band of twenty continued north, leaving their fellow travelers behind. Toothless Margaret stayed at Mary's side to help where she could, and more than once the people told Mary she was blessed with healing from God.

Mary smiled, thinking of how she would have found their words offensive at one time. Now she knew comfort from them and wondered if her father could have possibly known the same peace in his heart.

"You are marked by God to be a healer, child," Margaret told her as Mary mixed a balm.

"My father and grandmother were healers as well," Mary replied. "'Tis in our family."

The old woman nodded. "Where are ye bound with your brood?"

"North, to my grandmother's estate. She lives outside

of York."

"'Tis our good fortune and the hallowed Father's blessings to have crossed our paths with you and your man. We are too weak to care for ourselves properly, yet your man has seen to our needs for food and fire, while you have cared for our sicknesses."

Mary finished her task and got to her feet. "I am glad God saw fit to cross our paths, Margaret. He always seems to know just when to bring folk together."

"She has the Lady's touch," one man remarked to Margaret. "She should journey to the Lady of the Moors and join her in healing."

"God guides her steps as He does the Lady's. I would think if it be befitting for them to join, He will do the joining."

"I will go ahead and see if I can locate your grandmother's estates," Peter said to an exhausted Mary.

She struggled to keep her eyes open long enough to consume the bowl of stew Peter had placed in her hands.

"Gwenny is able to get about on her leg without too much interference, and Darias, Gideon, and Ellen have promised to see to the others. I should only be gone a few hours, maybe more, but I will be back before nightfall."

"When will you go?" Mary asked in a barely audible voice.

"At daybreak. I will see everyone fed and then be off."

Mary took one more drink of the rich broth and put the bowl down on the ground. "I need to rest," she murmured and stretched out beside the fire. She was sound asleep before Peter could bring a cover to place over her.

Peter watched her for some time and reflected on her concerns for his losses should he marry her. *But what of the gains, sweet Mary?* he thought. She had no means of realizing the value he placed on her.

A memory from another time came to Peter's mind. He could see the rich, jewel-encrusted gown of a newly-widowed duchess. It was impossible to remember her name, but Peter well remembered her words.

"You would be an amusement to me," she had whispered against his ear. "I would give you control of my lands, and you would give me whatever I asked for." The purring voice echoed in his ears. There had been others like her as well. Women who were selfish and greedy. Women who sought only to satisfy their own desires.

Peter looked again to Mary. Her lips were slightly parted and her cheeks, though pale, were illuminated by the flickering campfire. Sooty lashes fell against her skin, and ebony hair tumbled down around her shoulders in an alluring curtain.

It will be hard to leave her for London, he thought and made his bed on the opposite side of the fire. He glanced quickly to the wagon where all of the children were sleeping, crowded together for warmth. All was well, and a deep, saturating contentment washed over Peter. God was in His Heaven and all was well with the world.

Peter rode out the next morning as promised. He looked back several times and noted the sorrowful expression on Gideon's face.

"Hurry back, Papa!" Gideon called, and Peter's chest tightened in a way he could not explain. The boy had only taken to calling him that in the last few days, and even now, though it sounded foreign to his ears, it seemed quite appropriate in his heart.

With a wave, Peter nudged the horse into a gallop and went north to seek out the home of Lady Elizabeth Beckett. It was a well-known estate not far from York. By his best calculations, Peter knew they were no more than a day away from York, and it seemed natural that Lady Beckett's home would be nearer still.

His plan had been forming slowly, ever since he'd

decided to take Mary north under his protection. He would reach the estate first and break the news of Guy Beckett's death. Then he would speak to Lady Beckett of allowing Mary and the children to remain with her while he journeyed to London.

The country was a lonely one with rolling moors and marshy wastes. There, the wind blew straight down from the north and the wetness of it could chill a man in minutes. Peter tightened his grip on the reins and urged the horse to hasten.

The single beaten road made a fork, and remembering the instructions of the monks, Peter chose the left fork and pressed on. Before an hour had passed, he spied the rooftop of a huge stone manor house, and as he drew closer, the gray stone wall protecting the estate came into clear view.

The silent emptiness of the moors was soon behind him, even though the estate was planted firmly in their spaces. The grounds were filled with a multitude of people and activities. Dismounting, Peter led his steed through the clamoring people and made his way to the manor house door.

"Sylvia, take these new ones to the bathhouse and see that they are cleaned up and clothed," a silver-haired woman was saying. The young woman to whom she spoke, curtsied lightly and motioned the people to follow her.

The woman turned to enter the house, when Peter spoke. "Are you Lady Beckett?"

The woman stopped and noted Peter for the first time. "I am."

"I am Sir Peter Donne, servant to His Majesty King Edward III."

Elizabeth Beckett, a small woman who greatly resembled her granddaughter in facial appearance, smiled. "And how might I be of service to His Majesty's aid? What ailment do you boast, and how might I see to it?"

Peter looked at her with confusion. "I do not have an

ailment. Why do you ask?"

Elizabeth laughed. "Look around you. They all come here for healing. I presumed it must be so with you as well."

Peter did look around him and then the truth dawned on him. "You are the Lady of the Moors."

"I see you have heard the legends. Although I am no legend, and no mystical magic is woven here. Simple prayer and common sense with a pinch of the right herbs and tenderness is all I use."

"And so it is with your granddaughter Mary," Peter said, waiting to see what reaction might come from the older woman.

Elizabeth gasped and the color drained from her face. "Mary?"

Peter stepped forward to take hold of her arm. "Might I come in and explain?"

She nodded and led him into the house. Here, there was only the movement of servants, and Peter was grateful for the quiet.

Elizabeth motioned to a chair. "Please tell me what you know of my granddaughter."

Peter took a seat beside Lady Beckett. "Your granddaughter is well. She is nearby and making her way here."

"How can this be?"

Peter frown. "I'm afraid the news is not good. Your son Guy is dead."

Elizabeth clutched a hand to her throat. "Dead? Was it the fever?"

"I think it best Mary share her news of that with you. She knows it better, and I would only muddy the tale. There is more, however, which I can share, if you are up to it."

"Please," Elizabeth said in a near frantic tone. "Tell me all."

Peter relayed his first meeting of Mary and led Elizabeth through the tale of their growing entourage. "I left her with ten children and at least that many sick, just south of here."

"Harsh weather is due to set in. We must bring them all here," Elizabeth stated firmly. She was regaining her strength from the shock of Guy's death, Peter deemed.

"I saw the signs myself and feared a rain before I could even return. I will bring them here, but a wagon will be needed for the ill and injured."

"I have one," Elizabeth replied. "I have two in fact and will send one of my best groomsmen to aid you."

Peter got to his feet. "Lady Beckett, I have a strange request of you."

Elizabeth stared up questioningly as though his words had rooted her to her seat. "What is it?"

"I plan to marry your granddaughter as soon as I can journey to London and complete my business with the King. I have no doubt he will allow us to wed once he hears of my great love for her. I ask only that you allow Mary and the children to remain with you until I can prepare a place for them. I have no lands of my own at this time, but many has been the time when the King has promised them to me. I will simply put forth my request that his promise be realized."

Elizabeth got slowly to her feet and held out her hand. She took Peter's large, calloused hand in her own and smiled. "My child, you and Mary are welcome here for all time. The wee ones you are caring for will be welcomed as my own. You see for yourself, this is a place of healing and love. I could not turn away my own flesh. They are welcome here, as are you, for as long as needed."

Peter, with his hand still firmly held by Elizabeth, bowed low to show his respect. "You are a gracious lady," he whispered. "The stories I have heard of you were all true and more."

"Go quickly," Elizabeth said with tears in her eyes. "God go with you and safe journey. I will leave fires burning on the walls in order to guide you here."

fifteen

Mary heard the clatter of wagons and somehow knew that Peter was responsible. She saw in the purple twilight that not one, but two wagons were making their way toward the camp and that Peter's horse lazily tagged along behind the first.

When Peter jumped down from the wagon seat, Mary wanted nothing more than to run into his embrace, but at the moment her hands were greasy with ointment and the patient at her side was far more in need of her comfort than she was of Peter's.

Hurrying with her task, Mary felt Peter's presence before he spoke.

"I am nearly finished," she said softly, without bothering to look up.

"I have brought two wagons to transport these folk to your grandmother's estate."

"My grandmother!" Mary said and instantly left her work. "You have seen her? Truly?"

Peter's gaze was warm and loving. "Aye, I have seen her and she is well."

"What of me? Did you tell of me?" Mary asked, her voice betraying an anxious note.

"I did and she was most pleased." Peter reached out to take Mary's hand, but she quickly turned back to her patient.

"My hands are covered with balm. Give me a moment and I will wash them." She finished with the boil-infested man and walked to the water. Peter held out a towel when she stood again and instead of leaving her to dry her hands, he took up the task with a slow, methodic stroke.

"I told her of your father's passing," Peter said, gently rubbing her fingers between the material.

Mary nodded, feeling her pulse quicken from his actions. "I suppose 'twas most difficult for her to accept."

"Aye, she was deeply sorrowed at his passing. I did not tell her how he died. I thought perhaps it best to leave that to you."

Mary said nothing. She could only imagine this woman, her grandmother. What would she say to her when they first met? How could she explain the journey she'd taken and what she'd learned since that terrible night so long ago?

Her hands were more than dry, but still Peter continued rubbing them. Now, however, the towel had been discarded and it was Peter's own warm hands that covered hers.

In the background, Mary could hear the commotion of the sick being loaded into wagons, along with the sing-song excitement of the children as they too, prepared for the journey.

"My hands are dry," she whispered hoarsely, wanting very much to act as though his actions had not affected her.

"Aye," he whispered, still staring deeply into her eyes.

"We should be about our work. There is much to be done if we are to break camp this eve."

"Aye."

Mary felt him draw her close. His arms surrounded her with a circle of strength, and Mary cherished the moment and drew courage on from it for the future.

"What is she like?" Mary finally questioned.

"Your grandmother?"

"Aye. What is she like?"

"She is loving and gentle, like you." Peter's whispered words fell against her hair, and Mary couldn't help but sigh.

"And she is well?" Mary forced herself to ask.

"She is. And she looks forward to seeing you."

Mary allowed herself one more moment of Peter's embrace before she pulled away. "Then we'd best be about our way. I saw signs of rain, and the wind bespeaks of cold weather."

"'Tis the same thing your grandmother told me." He grinned at her. "Come along then. The sooner we get to Lady Beckett's, the sooner I can journey to London and get Edward's blessings on our union."

"You will go so soon?" Panic rose up in Mary. Unbidden tears formed in her eyes. It was only that she was so tired, she told herself. Tired and worried for those in her care. "What of the children? What of me?"

Peter took her hand and kissed it lightly. "Lady Beckett assures me we have a home with her for all time."

"The children as well?"

"Aye, the children as well. You will find your grandmother a most fascinating woman."

Peter was not wrong on that matter. Mary was amazed at the bustle of activity going on in the manor yard so long after night had darkened the skies to black.

They arrived with another group of travelers. One in their band stood ringing the gate bell and beseeching the house to allow them entry.

"What business have ye here?" an older gentleman asked the band of travelers.

"We seek the Lady," the man replied.

"Enter soul," the man said, pulling back the heavy wooden door. He immediately spied Peter and the wagons and motioned them through as well.

"We have expected your return, sire," the man told Peter. He turned and called to several others, and soon a bevy of people swarmed around the wagons.

"We have rooms in the building yonder," the man told Margaret. "Ye will be cared for by the Lady."

"Be ye speaking of the Lady of the Moors?" Margaret asked anxiously.

Mary was startled at the question and thought to offer Margaret the answer, but before she could speak, the old gatekeeper answered.

"Aye, the Lady is about the manor just now. She prepares for her granddaughter's arrival."

"My grandmother is the Lady of the Moors?" Mary asked no one in particular.

"Did I fail to mention that?" Peter questioned with a mischievous grin.

"Aye, did you leave out much else? Say perhaps that Edward is already taking up residence in the barn?"

Peter laughed out loud, causing the children to wake. "Nay, King Edward is not here, although I wish he were. 'Tis likely to be a cold night, and I would relish a wife at my side to keep me warm."

Mary felt her face grow flush and was grateful for the dim light of torch and campfire. "Your steed should make an ample companion," she teased and jumped down from the wagon. Taking up Anne in her arms, Mary looked to the manor house. "But if you do not mind so very much, Sir Knight, I would like an introduction first."

Peter climbed down from his mount and handed the reins to the gatekeeper. "I will happily make this presentation," he said, taking up Mary by the arm. "Gideon, Darias," he called over his shoulder, "you help the others down and follow us to the house."

Sleepily, the children began to move to the back of the wagon. Gwenny, who was now quite capable on her own, grabbed up Edward and followed after Mary and Peter as quickly as she dared. Like ducks waddling after their mother, the children fell into line. Now wide-eyed and fully alert to the new surroundings, all seemed eager to know of their new home.

In the doorway stood the figure of a woman, and Mary knew it would be her grandmother. Flashes of conversation between her father and herself came to mind. "My mother's love of religion and all its trappings outweighed her love for me." Mary remembered her father's sad voice speaking the words and suddenly she longed for his presence like never before. *If only they could have put their differences aside,* she thought silently. *If only.*

"Lady Beckett, may I present your granddaughter, Mary." Peter's voice feigned formality, but Mary knew he was quite at ease with the circumstances.

Elizabeth Beckett stepped forward and reached out to embrace Mary. She cried openly at the sight of her only granddaughter. "I have dreamed of this day, yet thought I would never live to see it. My heart is filled with such joy, little Mary."

Mary felt her apprehension melt away. "Grandmother," she whispered and buried her face in the aging woman's wimple.

Anne slept through the reunion, but the other children began clamoring about their empty stomachs.

"Come, come," Elizabeth said to the brood. "I have hot meat and bread by the fire. You can eat your fill."

Mary wiped her eyes and looked at Peter as her grandmother led the little ones away to eat. "Thank you, Peter," she said and stretched up on her toes to kiss his cheek.

"Why, Mary," he teased, "what a bold woman you are."

She smiled and shifted Anne in her arms. With a casual glance over her shoulder as she walked away, Mary replied, "'Tis a pity Edward is not in the barn."

The following dawn brought Mary and Elizabeth together to work on the sick and injured. There was much talk about the Italian fever, and Mary related to her grandmother how Guy Beckett had strived to find a cure.

"The fever has not been so great here in the moor country," Elizabeth told Mary. "'Tis a colder climate, and I believe less suitable to fevers. We do not suffer over much here, even with winter's cold upon us."

"My father believed a chill could make the fever worse. They would not allow bathing for the people who were exposed to the disease."

Elizabeth finished binding the wound of a young woman and turned to Mary with a gleam in her eye. "I was told you could catch the disease from lustful relations with old women."

Mary giggled. "That, my father did not mention in his journal."

"Journal? Your father kept a journal?"

"Aye, he had many. I brought them with me," Mary said, rewinding a strip of bandage cloth. "I will share them with you."

"Tell me of your father," Elizabeth said, motioning Mary to follow her. "Come, we will sit and share a few quiet moments."

Mary followed her grandmother back into the manor house and up the stairs to her private solar. Pointing to the canopied bed, Elizabeth took a seat at the head. "This will be most comfortable," she said, and Mary quickly agreed.

"Your Peter would not relay the death of your father. How came he to die, Mary?"

Mary was not prepared for this straight-forward questioning. "I despise the very memory of it."

"Please tell me," Elizabeth said in a pleading tone. "I must know the truth."

Mary settled back against the post of the canopy. "My father was a good man, although he found religion a grievous thing to bear. He spoke seldom of God or of the church."

"'Tis the man I remember," Elizabeth said with a sad smile.

"My father was a man of science. He studied long hours with colleges, even braving the church's retribution by performing dissections."

"Do tell!"

"'Tis true," Mary admitted. "I watched them from a hole in the floor of my room. I believe he knew I watched, for the positioning of the bodies was always such that my modesty would not be compromised. I worked at his side the rest of the time. 'Tis a fond memory for me indeed. He taught me the use of balms and potions, things that would aid the healing of sick and ease the miseries of the dying. I cherished those times with him, for he treated me as an equal and not merely a child."

"Was he a good father?" Elizabeth asked earnestly.

"Aye, I thought him the best," Mary replied. "He cared for me in the best ways possible, and I never wanted for anything. Even at the end. . ." Her mouth suddenly grew dry.

"Please, go on," Elizabeth urged.

"My father had arranged for a dissection. The body of a newly dead prison inmate was to be delivered and evaluated. The man had died from the plague and my father desired to continue his studies of plague victims in order that he might find a way to help those still living."

"What happened?"

"Two men brought the body in a chest, and apparently someone in the village learned of this. The villagers stormed the house, calling my father and his colleges to account for their sins. When my father went outside to meet them, I hurried to gather as much as I could and sneak out the back. I thought perhaps if the worst happened, I would be able to preserve a small bit of my father's work. At best, I could return the things and no one would be the worse for it."

"But things went badly?" Elizabeth questioned, yet her voice held a tone that told Mary she knew full well the answer.

"Aye. They called my father a consorter of the devil. They called me a witch and his friends were just as evil. They said we had caused the plague upon their village. My father's actions were deemed the reason for their children dying in mass."

"How awful for you, child." Elizabeth reached out an aged wrinkled hand and patted Mary's trembling one.

"My father had only sought to help them, Grandmother. He did not desire to see them hurt or dying."

"Of course not."

"He resented the church's interference. He felt God had abandoned him long ago. He felt that you had chosen God over him, and he could not bear the possibility that I might do the same."

Elizabeth's eyes filled with tears. "I told him 'twas no contest of God and man. God had His place and my child had another. Guy felt that if all my heart did not belong to him, then no fractioned part could either. I tried to explain that God's love surrounded us and came out through our love for others. I told him 'twas not a matter of him getting a lesser part of his mother's love, but that my love was only possible because God had loved me first."

"I see that now," Mary said softly, "but then, when my father spoke of his loss and the sadness he felt, I could only resent the God that took you away from him."

"Mary, God never took me away from your father. Guy did that. Guy took himself from me in a fit of rebellion and independent will. I never knew your mother and would probably not have heard of your birth had it not been for a kindly friend who journeyed south one year and spoke in person to your father."

"I was afraid to come north to you after his death," Mary admitted after several moments of silence. "I feared that perhaps my father's words had been correct. I feared you would not want me here."

Elizabeth held open her arms, and Mary went into them

like a child who had suffered a fall. "Oh, child," the older woman whispered, "I have wanted you near since I first heard of your birth. I love you and it gives me great pleasure to open my home, as well as my heart, to you."

"I thought I was all alone, but God keeps showing me ways in which I am most surely not."

"I think that He has perhaps given you more than just an aging old woman, am I right?" Elizabeth asked, her tone light and teasing.

Mary, reluctant to pull away, nodded her head against her grandmother's shoulder. "The children need me."

"'Twas not children I spoke of. What of your young man? What of Peter?"

Mary sat up at this. "What did he say of me to you?"

Elizabeth smiled, and her face grew radiant in her love for Mary. "He asked me to care for you while he journeyed to London. He asked before even bringing you here, just in the fear that I might say no."

"That would have presented a great problem, indeed." Mary's voice was thoughtful. "I had not thought of what a burden it would be upon a man such as Peter."

"Men think differently than women. At least it has been my observation that they do. Your grandfather, God rest his soul, was an even-tempered man with a heart for justice. But let something happen that threatened my well-being, and the man became fierce. Men concern themselves with things such as protection and preservation. Peter's concern is how to provide a home for you and the children. I sensed that more than heard it in the words he spoke. His first duty was to provide for you in whatever manner he could. With my acceptance of you and the children, he is now free to go out and conquer a more permanent arrangement."

Mary nodded absentmindedly. "I kept adding children to our number. I only thought of the love they needed or the fact that they were alone in the world, as was I. I never thought of how to feed them or what I would do to shelter and clothe them. I simply saw them and loved them."

"That is the balance in us, Mary. We show our love in different ways. Men show theirs in one and women in another, yet both are still love and still greatly needed. Children need both a mother and a father to nurture and grow them strong."

"I know that well, for my mother was dead long before I could understand the loss."

Elizabeth nodded. "I did not even know I carried a child when your grandfather was killed. I had these lands and the income that came from them, but I was certain it was all he had left me of himself. How joyful I was to learn of my mistake. Still, I knew it to be hard upon your father to grow up without a man to guide his days. Perhaps if he had known a father's love, he might never have rebelled so completely against God's love."

"I pray he chose the true way before his death," Mary said with a trembling voice.

"He knew full well the truth, Mary. I am sure when he saw his own death coming that he would not allow pride to keep him from God. We must pray it was so and leave it to the mercy of God. There is naught else we can do."

"But I want to see him in heaven," Mary protested. "I cannot imagine my contentment there without him."

Elizabeth tenderly brushed back a strand of ebony hair. "Trust God, Mary. His heaven is filled with joy, and no sorrow can live there. You will not go into His gates with a heavy heart."

Mary lay back against her grandmother and relished the comfort of feminine arms. She had never known a woman's touch. Never known a mother's love. Softly she began to sob for all that she had lost.

"You are home now, Mary. You are home."

sixteen

The following morning, Mary stretched leisurely from her bed and wondered at the quietness of her room. Where were the children? Where was Anne with her incessant morning cries for milk? For a moment Mary panicked, and then memory served to remind her she was in her grandmother's house. No doubt Lady Beckett had already seen to the comfort and needs of the children.

"Oh, Father in heaven," Mary began, "I am so blessed. Thank You for bringing us safely to this place. Thank You for my grandmother and her loving heart."

A knock on the door interrupted her prayer. "Come in," she called out and pulled the cover high.

"I feared you might sleep all day," Elizabeth said good-naturedly. "There is an anxious young man in the yard below. He prepares for his journey and would not be happy to leave without sharing a word with you."

Mary felt the color drain from her face. She leaped from the bed and pulled on her only clothes. "He is leaving?" she gasped the words. Dragging a brush through her thick black mane, Mary didn't even bother to braid or tie it back.

If her grandmother answered her, Mary never heard. She was compelled to be at Peter's side and fearful that she would find him already gone from the manor. Without thought for shoes, she hurried down the cold stone steps and out the front door.

Rains had come during the night, leaving everything saturated. Even now the skies threatened to pour again, and Mary shivered against the steady wind that blew down from the north.

"Mary Elizabeth!" her grandmother called from the door.

Turning, Mary saw the old woman hold out her shoes and a thick cloak. "Even without stockings," her grandmother began, "your feet will be happy to accept these."

Begrudgingly, Mary retraced her steps and put the shoes on her feet. Elizabeth wrapped the cloak around Mary and pointed to the barn. "He is in there."

"I wish King Edward were as well," Mary muttered.

Peter stood checking the feet of his horse when Mary entered the barn. She was terrified the feelings they had shared would somehow be dissipated by their arrival at the Beckett estate.

For a moment she said nothing, instead choosing to pull the thick blue wool closer to her body. Her black hair tumbled down in a frenzied veil, leaving her wild and gypsy-like in appearance. *There is too much I want to say,* she thought. *Too much I want to share. I know him not and now he is going away and perhaps I will never see him again.*

A lump came to her throat. *You are being a silly child,* she chided herself. But when she looked at the man before her, all Mary could think of was how she longed to keep him from going. *I will not cry and beg him to stay,* she promised. *I will not make this more difficult than it has to be. If he has changed his mind in the light of day, I will not make it impossible for him.*

She had nearly convinced herself to turn around and go, when Peter seemed to sense her presence and turned from the steed.

"Mary! I began to think I would have to drag you from that bed," he said with the laughing voice that Mary had come to appreciate.

He was dressed in a dark green tunic and leather cotehardie. His heavily muscled legs were clad in matching green wool with high knee boots that laced up the middle. His brown hair was carelessly combed, and his face newly shaven. It was all Mary could do to stay in place.

"Grandmother said you wished to tell me goodbye," Mary said, trying to force her voice to sound normal. *I will not cry,* she reminded herself.

"Aye, London calls," Peter said without giving his words much thought. He went back to checking the horse's hooves and added, "Your grandmother has agreed to keep you and the children here."

"Aye, she told me as much," Mary answered. In her mind she thought of velvet-clad ladies with their wily ways and titles. *I am but a physician's daughter. A woman without means or the ability to provide a dowry.* A fleeting thought reminded her that her grandmother was titled and owned the estate upon which she stood. But it wasn't Mary's land and title, and it certainly wasn't about to become hers any time soon. Maybe never.

"I will be back before you know it. I intend to deliver my report and plead our case before the King first thing. Barring any complications, which of course there is always the possibility of, I will return here with Edward's blessing to marry."

Mary barely heard the words. He was really going away. He would return to London and his life at court. He would taste good food upon fine china plates and enjoy the best drink available served in gold and silver goblets. He would sit beside sweet-smelling women in silks and satins. Women who would see his comely face and deem him a fair catch. She bit her lip hard to keep from crying out and begging him to stay.

She hadn't realized that Peter was watching her. Glancing up, she caught his quizzical stare as he leaned against the horse's stall.

"You are very quiet, sweet Mary. Pray tell what is going about in that very busy mind?"

Mary straightened a bit and pushed back her shoulders. Determined to remain emotionless, Mary tried to sound offended. "There are many sick people about me. I cannot very well stand here all day and not consider their needs."

Peter shook his head. "You lie. You are thinking not of the sick."

Mary swallowed hard. "I have much to think on. The children, my grandmother, and. . .and. . ." She could think of nothing else to say.

"And me? And the fact that I am leaving. Are you thinking of my departure and the distance I will place between us?"

Mary wanted to scream her affirmation, but instead she whirled around to leave. *If I stay, I will say something foolish,* she thought. *If I stay, I will cry and I will plead and it will be the most regrettable thing I have ever done.*

"Stop right there, Mary!"

The authoritative manner in which Peter called out, left her little choice but to halt. Wishing she could lose herself in the heavy cloak, Mary held her breath and waited for what Peter would say next. *If I do not look at him, mayhap I will keep myself from tears.*

"Mary, come here."

His voice was compelling, but Mary remained rigidly planted to her spot. She drew a deep breath. So far, so good. Just a few more minutes and he would leave. Just a few more precious seconds of shared time together, and he would ride away from her and take her heart with him.

His touch was her undoing. Peter's hands upon her cloaked shoulders caused Mary to begin shaking so hard it made her teeth chatter.

"Are you cold?" he asked softly, turning her to face him.

"No!" she exclaimed and tried to wrench away.

"But you are trembling," he said sympathetically. "Come, I will see you to the. . ." His words fell away as he lifted her chin with his finger. "You are not cold."

The statement and the look in his eyes told Mary he'd guessed her innermost thoughts. With a knowing smile he swept her into his arms and kissed her so ardently that Mary's feet left the floor. She could barely steady herself to keep from falling flat when he released her.

"Think you that I could share this affection and leave you without another thought? I might once have been such a cad, but that was before the truth of God was within me."

Mary shook her head. "I know very little of the man you were, or for that matter, the man you are."

"Have my actions not told you of my love? Has the life lived before you not spoken louder than any tale of the past?"

Mary tried hard not to think of the aching in her heart. She tried hard to remember the wonder of his touch only moments before. *If I think on these things, I will fall apart.*

"You are a man of honor, Peter Donne," she finally spoke.

"And I have given you a pledge of love, a promise to marry, and my word that I will return. What more would you have of me?" he asked her seriously.

A sob broke from deep within, and Mary turned to flee his presence. Peter would have none of it, however, and caught her by the cloak and whirled her back around.

"Leave me be," she begged and pushed him away as he took her in his arms. "I cannot bear this one second more."

"Ah, Mary," he whispered against her ear. "Please believe in me."

His pleading tone caused her to stop fighting, and when Mary lifted her gaze to his, she found tears in his eyes.

"Yes," she said softly. Stretching to reach his lips with

her own, Mary kissed him with all the love she felt for him inside.

"You are mine, sweet Mary. You are mine, as I am yours."

"Aye," Mary said, believing it to be so. She wiped at her tears with the back of her hand. "I am yours."

Watching her walk away was the hardest thing Peter had yet to do. He had fought battles in France, watched scores of people die from the plague, and journeyed hundreds of miles across nations in the name of his king. But all these challenges paled in the face of this moment. His heart told him he was a fool to leave, yet there was no other choice.

Climbing onto his horse, Peter cast a quick glance at the children who stood anxiously at the gate. Darias and Gideon were trying hard not to cry, while Gwenny sobbed and cradled a distracted Edward much too tightly. The others were somber but at least did not cry, and for this Peter was grateful.

"I will bring you something from London," he promised, and the faces of the little ones seemed brighter.

A steady drizzle had begun, and the longer he lingered, the harder it seemed to rain.

"I will ride hard and return in a fortnight," he called to Mary. He doubted the truth of his words, knowing the roads would be saturated and the passage slow. Should he tell Mary of the possible difficulties and further worry her? Saying nothing more, he waved and gave the horse his head.

❧

Christmas Eve arrived, and still Peter had not returned to the Beckett estate. Mary was devastated. Surely something had happened to him. He might even have fallen victim to the plague fever and she would never know that he had died.

Restlessly, she tried to put her fears from her mind and join in the festivities of the season. The huge yule log was brought in and placed in the oversized hearth in her grandmother's dining hall. It would burn for the twelve days of Christmas until Epiphany arrived to mark the coming of the wisemen.

Outside, rain continued to make a daily appearance, leaving the fields standing in puddles of icy cold water. The manorial servants were given these days away from regular work, and an atmosphere of celebration lightened the hearts of even the harshest soul. Elizabeth had seen to the decorations of holly and ivy in the great hall of her manor, while in the kitchen a grand feast was in order to make the celebration even finer.

The children had been given new clothing, a gift from their Grandmother Elizabeth, as well as a toy. The boys were happy to play with carved wooden swords, and the girls were given dolls dressed in soft, white gowns.

Mary tried to show a festive spirit. She dressed in the bright red velvet gown her grandmother had chosen for her. She even managed to arrange her hair in a fashionable style and trimmed her hair-covering with bits of holly and ivy. But there was an emptiness in Peter's absence that kept her from true joy.

When the tenants of Elizabeth's estate began to arrive for the annual Christmas feast, Mary dismissed herself to the privacy of her bedroom and prayed. "I know 'tis the celebration of Your Son's birth," she began, tears falling in steady streams from her face, "and I know for the first time what it is to honor this day for that reason. But Father, my heart is sorely vexed and the reason is well-known to You. I fear for Peter, Father. I fear that he has fallen ill or worse yet, has died."

She spoke the words and even then realized that more fearful still was the possibility that Peter had simply decided not to return to York.

Downstairs, Mary could hear the singing and laughter,

but her heart would not be comforted. A light knocking caused her to wipe her eyes and take a deep breath.

"Come in," she called.

Gideon appeared to peek his head around the door.

"Why are you here, Mama?" he questioned, and Mary felt a bit of the sting leave her heart.

"I thought to pray a moment." It was completely true, Mary reasoned. No need for Gideon to know her fears.

"You are worried about Papa," the boy said, closing the door behind him. "You should not worry, God goes with him."

"Aye, I know 'tis true," Mary said, realizing that keeping her heart from the boy would be impossible. "Still, it has been so long."

"Grandmother said it had been only a month and that with the heavy rain we should not worry." His face was filled with innocence and love.

Mary knelt, opened her arms, and held the boy against her for a moment. He seemed so grown up in his miniature cotehardie of blue wool. Had not her grandmother spoken just the night before on the faith of children? Children, she had told Mary, were invested with the ability to believe with all their hearts. They trusted their parents, never wondering whether or not they would provide or remain to care for them. God asked that we come to Him as a little child with faith that He would remain true to His Word. How very hard that was, Mary deemed.

"He will come back," Gideon said softly, and leaning up he kissed her cheek. "You will see. Papa is a man of his word. He promised he would never leave me, and I believe him."

Mary pulled Gideon away for just a moment. Yes, she could see the truth of his words in the warm glow of his eyes. He held no doubt, but then Gideon was a child and he did not know the ways of riches and wanton women.

"You go on below and play the games with your new brothers and sisters. We are a family now, and we should celebrate as one. I will come below in just a moment."

Gideon smiled broadly. "Grandmother said we could have the wastel loaves." He spoke of the traditional game of finding the bean inside a loaf of bread. Whoever found the bean was king for the feast. "I hope I find it."

"And what will you decree as king?"

Gideon looked thoughtful for a moment. "I will call for sweet pies to be served all day."

"Oh, Gideon," Mary laughed and sent the boy on his way.

When Mary came below, the children rushed to her side. The little ones held up their arms to be picked up, while Anne on a blanket in front of the fire was sitting up grinning at Mary. *How quickly she has grown,* Mary thought.

"She has progressed quickly," Elizabeth said, echoing Mary's thoughts as she crossed to her side. The revelry in the hall nearly drowned out her words. Both women studied Anne for a moment.

"I feel as though she has always been my own," Mary said, laughing at the way the baby tumbled over while studying her own fingers and toes. "Do you think it wise to leave her out of swaddling so soon?"

"Bah!" Elizabeth replied. "I have never cared for the idea of binding children until they are struggling to move about. I think the earlier they do flex those little limbs, the sooner they grow strong and healthy. Do not fear, Mary, Anne is fairly shining with health."

Gwenny came to Mary's side, her limp barely noticeable. "Mary, will you come and share the wastel?"

Mary glanced at the children's eager faces. "Of course. And if I do not win today, then perhaps I will win tomorrow on Christmas."

"There are twelve chances for the twelve days," Darias reminded her.

"And the Three Kings Bread on Epiphany," Grandmother Elizabeth declared. "I always put a coin in that loaf to remind us that the wisemen brought gifts of gold to the Christ child."

"A real coin?" three children chanted in unison. "And we may keep it if we find it?"

"Of course," Elizabeth said, her eyes fairly dancing. "Now you children go and play. Mary and I must check on the sick, but we will be back before you know it."

Taking hold of Mary's arm, Elizabeth led her from the room and out the back of the house. "You seem to be in good spirits when you are with the children."

"I love them so," Mary admitted. "I suppose I never really considered what it would mean to be a mother and care for a child. I was always so busy with father that I never considered marriage and a family of my own. Father needed me to care for him, and a husband seemed unimportant."

"And now?"

Mary looked at her grandmother, knowing full well the older woman understood her fears and misery in Peter's absence. "Now it is most important. Love is a terrible and awful thing, as it is a wondrously joyful thing. Just when I believe myself to understand the matter, it baffles and confuses me until I am nearly dizzy in my contemplations."

Elizabeth laughed out loud. Pausing outside the door to the sickroom, she reached her hand to Mary's face. "'Tis always the way with human love. The road is one that not only takes us to the mountain, but plunges us deep into the valley. God's love, however, is the one type of love that never changes. His love is constant, and when human love fails us, His love will continue."

"If only I had the faith of the children," Mary wished.

"'If only' is a key that opens a door to regret," Elizabeth chided gently. "You cannot spend your life wishing that you had chosen another path. It will not change the first choice and it will not offer comfort on the journey forward. You can spend your life in regrets, Mary Elizabeth, or you can put your best foot forward and trust that you are making choices based on the influence of God's guiding hand."

"Oh, Grandmother, I am so blessed to have you. God was good to bring us together," Mary said, embracing the woman tightly. "If only. . ." She paused and issued a giggle. "'Tis an easy statement to give." Mary pulled back to see her grandmother's amused face. "I would have said, if only I had been allowed to grow up within your care, how very different things might now be."

"Just remember, Mary, in trading one life for another, we cast away all the good and lovely things we would have known in the first. Would you have traded your father's devotion and the time spent learning at his side?"

"Never!"

"Then mayhap we should trust that the very best has come to pass in each instance."

"Aye," Mary said with sudden understanding. "And more good is yet to come."

seventeen

New visitors to Beckett Manor continued to arrive even through the twelve days of Christmas. Epiphany came and went with Gideon the happy recipient of the "king's coin." He pledged to take everyone into town and buy gifts for all. Mary didn't have the heart to tell him the coin would not stretch quite that far.

It was on the Monday after Epiphany, Plow Monday, as it was called, that Mary found herself warmly dressed and standing in the fields of her grandmother's estates. Today there were contests to see how many furrows each man could plow. Whatever soil he was able to break would be his when true plowing time came at Candlemas in February.

Mary laughed at the sight and joined in with the others to cheer the group of villeins on with their work. It was a festive day and would mark the end of the Christmas celebration. Spying a new set of travelers, Mary left the festivities and made her way to the woman and child at the gate.

"My little one is suffering from a burn," her mother told Mary. "She was scalded by a caldron of water."

Mary gently took the child from her mother and motioned with her head to the place where the sick were kept. "Come with me and we will tend her."

Mary was unprepared for the hideous sight of the child's back and side. The reddened flesh was festering and peeling, and Mary feared that the child would succumb to her wounds.

"I will call the Lady of the Moors to help me," Mary said. "Keep her quiet, and I will return shortly."

Mary went out from the building in search of her

grandmother. A wave of nausea at the memory of the child washed over her. How terrible for the poor little waif to bear up under such a burden!

She found Elizabeth handing out pieces of candied fruits to the congregation of children from her estate. "Grandmother, there is child who is quite gravely ill. Her mother has brought her, and I have her in the sickhouse."

Elizabeth nodded and gave the bag over to one of the servants to finish the task. "What is her condition?"

"She has been hideously burned. The wounds are festering, and I know not if she will live."

Elizabeth nodded and made her way to the sickhouse. Throwing off her cloak, she went to the worried mother and tiny, lifeless girl.

"Mary, bring fresh well water, cold and clear."

Mary did as she was bid, and when she returned, Elizabeth was placing a spoonful of something in the child's mouth. "'Twill make her sleep, for the treatment will be most painful."

The mother of the child seemed to weaken at the thought, and Mary led her away to sit on a chair outside the room.

"First we will cleanse the burns with water, then with wine," Elizabeth told Mary. "I find greater healing when I wash a very bad wound, such as a burn, with a good stout wine."

The two women worked side by side to master the situation. Elizabeth removed pieces of burnt skin, and when all had been cleansed to her satisfaction, she directed Mary to bring a clean cloth of linen.

"We will soak this in a mixture of rose oil and essence of peony. I will add a bit of poppy oil as well, and we will cover the worst of the burns with the cloth. This should stay moist for three days. We will also need to keep the child resting, so administer a teaspoon of this every mealtime with a cup of broth."

"Will she live?" Mary asked hopefully.

"We will pray it so," Elizabeth said, placing her hand upon the child's brow. "She is such a tiny mite, but she seems quite strong."

They finished with the child, and after instructing the mother, made their way back to the celebration.

"'Tis hard to see the little ones suffering so," Mary said, absentmindedly.

"We do what we can, Mary, and trust God for the rest."

"It would seem trust is the one thing God is working to teach me most earnestly."

"Has He made progress with you yet?" Elizabeth teased.

"Aye, but 'tis no easy battle."

Realizing she'd left her cloak back in the sickroom, Elizabeth turned back.

Mary put a restraining hand on Elizabeth's arm. "I will fetch it for you, Grandmother. Stay here with your people." She hurried away before her grandmother could stop her. Truth be told, Mary longed for a few quiet moments to pray at the child's bedside.

"There is warm food in the house," Mary instructed the child's mother. "I will wait here a moment with your daughter while you get something to eat." The woman's eyes grew wide as though she could not believe her good fortune. "Go now," Mary urged, "and return here with your plate."

The woman had no sooner left than Mary bowed her head and prayed in earnest for the child. It was the first time Mary had truly given a patient over in prayer. How different it felt from the times when she had only her medicines and father's teachings to rely upon.

"'Tis in your hands now, Father," she whispered and noted that the child breathed evenly and without pain.

Turning to leave, Mary clasped her hand to her mouth to keep from crying out. Peter stood in the door not five feet away, resplendently dressed in the garb of court.

"Surely you are not adding another to our number, sweet Mary," he said with a grin.

"Peter!" she gasped his name, and mindless of who might see, she threw herself into his arms and covered his face with kisses. "Oh, Peter!"

His arms went around her waist and held her tightly against him. Mary could scarcely allow herself to believe the moment had finally come. Surely this was just another dream, she told herself and then pulled back to assure herself it was all very real.

"You are truly here," she whispered.

"Aye," he replied softly. "Had you given over to despair of ever seeing me again?"

Mary took on a look of surprise in order to keep from betraying her real feelings. "Of course not!"

Just then, the child's mother returned, and Mary quickly pulled Peter into the manor yard. She was stunned to find an entourage of men being directed by her grandmother to where they could seek shelter. She looked to Peter with a quizzical stare.

"They are mine," he answered her unspoken question. "Edward has sent them to help me establish our lands."

"Our lands?" Mary questioned, but just then Elizabeth called out a greeting.

"Peter, you are answered prayer," she said embracing him in a motherly fashion.

"As were you for me. I trust Mary has not overstayed her welcome here."

"Never!" Elizabeth declared. "She and the children have been purely a joy. I would keep you all beside me forever."

"Well, you shall nearly have your wish," Peter said, pulling from his cloak a leather satchel. "I have here Edward's permission to marry your granddaughter," he announced with a sly look at Mary's surprised face. "Do not look so surprised, sweet Mary, 'tis the main reason I returned to London."

Before he could continue, Peter found himself surrounded by the children.

"Papa!" Gideon called over and over, and the little ones mimicked him.

"Papa! Papa!" they chanted.

"Nothing has ever sounded sweeter," Peter said, hugging the little bodies close to his. "My, but you look so fine in your new clothes. Were these gifts from Christmas?"

"Yes," Gideon stated excitedly. "Grandmother had them made for us. Did you bring us a present from London?"

"That I did. More than one. First and most important is something I was just telling your grandmother and Mary. King Edward has given permission for Mary and me to wed and care for you as our own children."

Cheers went up from the older children, which in turn caused the younger ones to clap their hands and dance around.

"I told you he would come back, Mama," Gideon said, taking Mary's hand in his own. "I told you."

Mary smiled down at the boy. "Aye, you told me well, Gideon." Glancing up, she noted Peter held a questioning look on his face. "Now what else were you to tell us, sire?"

Peter held up the satchel. "Edward has given me the adjoining lands to the west of your grandmother's estate. We will be neighbors, Lady Beckett."

"What joy! I have long prayed for this day," Elizabeth said, and tears of happiness fell freely from her eyes. "You must have struggled long to get here. Your men told me of the many perils you faced. Come to the house and warm up and eat. You can tell us everything there."

The children, including Gideon, were already pulling Peter along to the house, chanting their stories of all that had happened in his absence. Arm in arm, Mary followed with Elizabeth.

"Now I will never be without my family," Mary said softly. "You will be near to me, and we can help one another."

"I truly meant it when I said this is answered prayer," Elizabeth replied. "I have long wondered to whom I would leave these lands. I hated to imagine they would simply fall back into the hands of the crown, only to be issued out to those who knew me not."

"Please do not speak of leaving for any reason," Mary admonished. "I want to know your company for a great many years. I have much to make up and much to learn from you."

&

The children had long been asleep in their beds and the candles and lamps extinguished to shine another day, when Peter and Mary finally found themselves alone.

Sitting before the low-burning fire, Mary reached out to warm her hands, while Peter finished sharpening his knife. She suddenly felt shy and uncomfortable. Stealing sidelong glances, she watched Peter work, still amazed that he was truly here in the same room. Outside the wind howled in a mournful reminder of winter's gripping cold and Mary shuddered.

"Are you cold?" Peter asked thoughtfully, putting the knife to rest beside the whetstone.

"A little," she answered, wondering what he would think if she told him of her discomfort.

Peter retrieved a heavy wool shawl he'd seen Elizabeth use earlier. "This should help," he said, placing it around her shoulders. His hands lingered to pull her hair free from the shawl, and Mary trembled at his touch.

For several moments, the only sound was that of the wind outside and the tiny pops and crackles of the wood on the grate. Mary fought to steady her nerves, while Peter remained at her back, his hands in her hair.

"So you thought I would not return." It was more statement than question. His voice sounded a little sad, and Mary
stiffened, wondering how to respond.

"Why do you say that?" Mary asked hesitantly. She knew
full well Gideon's words earlier in the day had prompted
such a response, but she was not yet certain how to speak
on the matter.

Peter came around to join her on the bench. "My love for
you is quite real, Mary." He looked at her with such pleading that Mary had to look away. "You were ever on my mind.
You and the children rode with me wherever I went. All I
could think of was you."

"I did not mean to fret," Mary finally said. She looked
ahead into the fire. "'Tis simply that I have never loved a
man, and I know naught of the ways of such a union." She
felt her face grow hot. "We pledged ourselves to marriage
without knowing much of each other."

"People are married in that manner quite often. Why, my
own mother was pledged to my father at the age of nine.
She knew nothing of him. When they were wed, she was
but thirteen years old, and still she only knew that he was of
a proper house, befitting her station."

"I am certain you speak the truth," Mary replied, "but I
am not familiar with such things. I was sheltered away. I
cared for my father, cooked and cleaned, sewed, and worked
at his side. I knew the love of a father to his daughter, and
romantic love seemed a world away and unimportant. Now,"
she said, reluctantly looking at Peter's tender expression,
"I find this love to be a confusing thing."

He reached out his hand. "How be that, sweet Mary?"

Mary put her other hand over his. "I had never known
jealousy until my heart belonged to you. Now, all I can imagine is the life you knew before and the women who would

take you away."

Peter surprised her by laughing, and Mary pulled her hand away and got to her feet. "'Tis not funny. How can you laugh when I have shared my heart with you?"

"I am sorry, Mary. I only find it humorous to imagine that any other woman could compel me to leave you."

"How is that so?" Mary stuck out her lower lip in a definite pout. She was not yet ready to concede that his laughter was justified.

"Mary," Peter said, getting to his feet, "'tis true enough that I have play the rogue and toyed with the affections of many. I have lived a life I am not proud of and have sought God's forgiveness for the harm I have caused. As a knight of the King, I knew wealth and adventure and certainly found myself among a great many beautiful women—"

"See then," Mary interrupted, "I am right to feel this way."

"Nay," he whispered with a finger to her lips. "There is no one between us except that which you place there. If only you will trust me, Mary, I will be the finest of husbands. I will pledge you my devotion, my love, and my loyalty."

Mary seemed to awaken to these words. "Grandmother said that 'if only' was a key to the door of regret. I suppose I see her meaning from my own wishes. I kept telling myself, if only we'd known each other longer or if only I were a lady of means."

"You would not have liked the man I used to be," Peter assured her. "But that man is no longer a concern. I am reborn through God's love and our Saviour's sacrifice. I am grateful that you knew me not when I was younger."

Mary began to feel a wave of peace wash over her. God had given them both rebirth from the old, selfish creatures they once were. "I love you, Peter," she said, reaching out her hand to his face. "That love frightens me a bit, for I know naught of how to be a wife or mother."

Peter pulled her into his arms and sighed. "Your loving heart has already made you capable of both tasks. Now put aside your fear and let trust come to life." He kissed her tenderly, and Mary felt herself giving into the warmth of their embrace. When Peter raised his head, he stared down at her with fiery brown eyes. "We need no longer wish for Edward to be in residence in the barn; he has granted his consent."

Mary smiled impishly. "Did you tell Edward of your ready-made family?"

"I did," Peter joined her teasing air. "He asked if I thought ten was quite enough or should I like to take a few more back with me from London."

"And what did you tell him?"

"I declined, believing that someone else should know the joy which had befallen me. I made it clear that ten was a hearty number and more than enough for a new knight and his lady fair."

"But what of our own children?" She questioned, releasing him in mock concern. "I'd always heard it told children were a sign of a healthy love between a man and woman."

Peter grabbed her around the waist and pulled her back. "Then we will surely double the number," he said with a mischievous wink, "for my love of you is. . ." He kissed her forehead. "Quite. . ." He kissed her nose. "Healthy." He kissed her mouth soundly.

Mary sighed and wrapped her arms around his neck. No longer were there doubts or lingering thoughts of "if only." There were no regrets in the love she felt for this man or in the heavenly love God had given her.

After a long, passionate kiss, Mary weakly pulled away and grinned. "There is a friar in the guest house," she whispered. "He came for the holiday celebration, and Grandmother thought it wise to keep him handy."

Peter caught her hand and pulled her to the door. "And you have kept this to yourself all this time? If only you would have spoken sooner, sweet Mary. If only. . ."

A Letter To Our Readers

Dear Reader:

In order that we might better contribute to your reading enjoyment, we would appreciate your taking a few minutes to respond to the following questions. When completed, please return to the following:

Rebecca Germany, Managing Editor
Heartsong Presents
P.O. Box 719
Uhrichsville, Ohio 44683

1. Did you enjoy reading *If Only*?
   ❑ Very much. I would like to see more books
      by this author!
   ❑ Moderately
      I would have enjoyed it more if _____

   _____

2. Are you a member of **Heartsong Presents**? ❑Yes ❑No
   If no, where did you purchase this book? _____

   _____

3. What influenced your decision to purchase this
   book? (Check those that apply.)

   ❑ Cover   ❑ Back cover copy

   ❑ Title   ❑ Friends

   ❑ Publicity   ❑ Other_____

4. How would you rate, on a scale from 1 (poor) to 5
   (superior), the cover design? _____

5. On a scale from 1 (poor) to 10 (superior), please rate the following elements.

___Heroine ___Plot

___Hero ___Inspirational theme

___Setting ___Secondary characters

6. What settings would you like to see covered in **Heartsong Presents** books?_____

_____

_____

7. What are some inspirational themes you would like to see treated in future books?_____

_____

_____

8. Would you be interested in reading other **Heartsong Presents** titles? ❑ Yes ❑ No

9. Please check your age range:
   ❑ Under 18 ❑ 18-24 ❑ 25-34
   ❑ 35-45 ❑ 46-55 ❑ Over 55

10. How many hours per week do you read? _____

Name _____

Occupation _____

Address _____

City_____ State_____ Zip_____

Joy to the World

Colleen L. Reece
Anita Corrine Donihue

This special gift book is a treasury of holiday stories, reminiscences, ideas, prayers, poetry, recipes, and more! Bring the joy of the holiday season into your home with traditions you can make your own as you celebrate the joy of Christ's birth with your family and friends.

64 pages, Hardbound, 5" x 6 ½"

·········Presents·······

Great Inspirational Romance at a Great Price!

Heartsong Presents books are inspirational romances in contemporary and historical settings, designed to give you an enjoyable, spirit-lifting reading experience. You can choose wonderfully written titles from some of today's best authors like Peggy Darty, Colleen L. Reece, Tracie J. Peterson, VeraLee Wiggins, and many others.

When ordering quantities less than twelve, above titles are $2.95 each.

Hearts♥ng Presents
Love Stories Are Rated G!

That's for godly, gratifying, and of course, great! If you love a thrilling love story, but don't appreciate the sordidness of some popular paperback romances, **Heartsong Presents** is for you. In fact, **Heartsong Presents** is the *only inspirational romance book club*, the only one featuring love stories where Christian faith is the primary ingredient in a marriage relationship.

Sign up today to receive your first set of four, never before published Christian romances. Send no money now; you will receive a bill with the first shipment. You may cancel at any time without obligation, and if you aren't completely satisfied with any selection, you may return the books for an immediate refund!

Imagine. . .four new romances every four weeks—two historical, two contemporary—with men and women like you who long to meet the one God has chosen as the love of their lives. . .all for the low price of $9.97 postpaid.

To join, simply complete the coupon below and mail to the address provided. **Heartsong Presents** romances are rated G for another reason: They'll arrive *Godspeed!*